Brookside Review

A Collection From the Brookside Writers Workshop

Netherstoned Press

Brookside Review: A Collection From the Brookside Writers Workshop

"Atopo" and "Anxiety" are excerpted from *Another Love Discourse,* a lyric novel by Edie Meidav, Terra Nova Press/MIT Press 2022, distributed by Penguin. The photo of Roland and Henriette Barthes was originally published in *Roland Barthes on Roland Barthes*, 1977, from the collection of Michel Salzedo.

Columbus: Lost in Paradise Chapter 1, by Dan Eeds, was first published in *Dull Pencil Anthology of YA Short Fiction* © 2014.

This is a compilation of fiction and non-fiction work. In the case of fiction, names, characters, businesses, events and incidents are the products of each author's imagination. Any resemblance to actual persons, living or dead, or actual events is purely coincidental. In the case of non-fiction, the events are true to the best of each author's memory. The authors in no way represent any company, corporation, or brand, mentioned herein. While we feel ourselves to be a collective, in this volume each author had complete autonomy, and as such, the views expressed in each work are solely those of the author and do not represent the combined views of any single other author nor our group.

Cover and book design by Megan Schiller
The cover art is an illustration of 40 Brookside Avenue in Berkeley, where the Brookside Writers met for many years.

Netherstoned Press
netherstonedpress.com

ISBN: 979-8-218-00584-9

To our mentor and hero, Mae Z. Meidav — she will live forever in our hearts and writing.

Contents

Introduction

By Michael C. Healy

For some 30 years now, the Brookside Writers Workshop has been meeting weekly, its participants finding a nourishing and stimulating outlet for creative expression. The work of the writers, who come from various walks of life and vocations, encompasses short stories and novels, poetry and plays, essays and travelogues. This volume, our first printed collection, takes the reader on a magical ride through time and space as we present pieces rising from both deep personal experience and realms unlived.

The founder of the workshop, Mae Ziglin Meidav, passed away on January 10, 2020, at the age of 84. A dynamo who led a multifaceted and artistic life, she was an engineer, a belly dancer, an actor and a director, and a produced playwright (with a PhD in sociology to boot). Her primary theme for the workshop was the concept of *writing as transformation;* the motto reflected her belief that in each of us there is something to say lurking just below the surface, waiting to be uncovered and shared. A tireless advocate of the creative process, she coached the workshop right up to her passing, even from her bed.

Mae started the workshop as an extracurricular lunchtime activity at the Oakland, California, offices of BART (the Bay Area Rapid Transit District), where she worked as a systems engineer for many years. The class attracted aspiring writers not only from BART, but from other agencies that were housed in the same government complex.

Once retired, Mae reconvened the group around the long dining room table at her spacious and stately house at 40 Brookside Avenue in Berkeley, California — picking up new acolytes as the years rolled on. Simultaneously she operated a small, independent theater company out of her home, the Brookside Repertory Theatre, and the writers workshop became an adjunct to that enterprise, taking on the Brookside name and a new emphasis on gearing the writing for the stage.

Each workshop session, which usually ran a couple of months, culminated with a reading or performance of the writers' pieces before an audience. Mae tapped her extensive network of professional actors to bring the works alive, and served as the producer, director and impresario of these legendary soirées.

Because this workshop has played such an important part in the lives of the writers, it has continued to meet weekly, organized by the members themselves. It is a testament to Mae and the energy and inspiration she brought to the table that the workshop has continued to flourish — and survived the challenges of meeting virtually during the pandemic. It is in honor of Mae's spirit and devotion to the workshop that the following works have been published in this review.

We are especially pleased to present a pair of pieces from Mae's daughter Edie Meidav, a prolific author who is a professor in the MFA Program for Poets and Writers at the University of Massachusetts, Amherst. Over the years, Edie would from time to time serve as a guest moderator for the Brookside Writers Workshop during her visits to the Bay Area, and we are thrilled and grateful that she has contributed to this volume excerpts from her new lyric novel, *Another Love Discourse.*

Our work as a community began years ago, and it continues in your reading of this anthology. It is our hope that you will find in these pages the delight of sharing stories that has been our gift all these years, and kindling for your own creative spark.

— Michael C. Healy, on behalf of the Brookside writing community

Gigi Benson

A Life Full of Incident:
A Memoir in the Making

By Gigi Benson

Scarlet Desire

By Gigi Benson

The deep seduction of oleanders, with a quiet permeating scent of silent security and seclusion deep within their depths. Where anyone could lose all sense of time, family and purpose. Gone. No trail. No scent beyond the sweet sour smell of a ripe pink grapefruit ready to drop in the palm of your hand. Who would know the fairies had taken you?

So green, the misplaced palms, or fronds, whatever they were called, they definitely were the most exotic leaves to lie between the sand track three-bedroom homes of the desert any imaginative mind could want and the lazy miles of citrus groves some drunk developers gambled away.

If you climbed over the cool cement walls between us and the grapefruit groves, lit out across the back of the neighbors' humongous pool and slid down behind the landscapers' curtain of oleanders you were alone. Beyond the twilight zone, beyond the bullies, safe in never-never land ... just a little hotter ... till you got 12 feet down where the hard brown dirt turned soft and cool.

A scream's throw from the irrigation canals, where crawdads and the lone cottonwood trees sucked the cool stream's song from its cradle, you could hide.

It's here I took Jonny Greenband to kiss me.

He had no idea what he was in for.

Running from the crew of kids, screaming for Reese's Pieces when they only came in tin foil cups ... long before the penny candy market came along and stale paper tempered their taste.

We hid. The older kids climbing across the tops of the grapefruit trees, like mindless monkeys they loped along in sixth-graders' supremacy while we cowered in our second-grader shadows.

Jonny turned to me, delighted at our hideaway ... feeling oh so brave and gallant for finding a spot safe from the bullies whooda certainly tanned his overstuffed hide in a shame he'd never survive.

We slid down the wall, grabbing grapefruits off their stems, plopping simultaneously to the cool sweet smell of soft dirt, pushing our bare feet before us as we ripped into the grapefruit's rind, pulling it back and dropping two front teeth deep into the sweet soft sinews of its bittersweet pink flesh.

We were seven and a half, sweltering in an Arizona summer orchard.

What did we know.

He was the biggest boy in our new school, looked like a fourth grader practically. Everyone said his dad was rich. He was funny and even more, he was the nicest kid we'd met all summer. He had black hair and dark eyes. Mom said his parents were divorcing, they were Jewish. I thought that meant they weren't Republicans.

He didn't mind I was the skinniest freckled-faced girl going into Mrs. Miller's third-grade class. "You're just a real short Pippi Longstocking," he'd said as he pulled me off my mangled bike the first time we met.

We laughed in innocence at our escape, victorious in eluding the older hooligans. He turned, looked me straight in the eye and we shared the moment of triumph.

The sixth graders sped by on their banana seat bikes, popping wheelies and screaming at little kids in their way, scaring the heebie-jeebies out of anyone in earshot with the playing cards clicking between their wheel spokes spattering the silence surrounding our simple neighborhood and never even looking at the hedges.

We'd outsmarted SIXTH GRADERS!

Then, feeling the reckless bravado that only a rambunctious precocious second grader can process, the soundtrack of some thundering movie swelled inside my head, and Vivien Leigh inhabited my body, Scarlett's potato-picking ivory pinky pulling my smock string from my jumper to bare my clavicles in victory.

"Kiss me," I hissed, "on my neck!"

The sun dappled through the leaves, every atom stopped in slow motion to witness my wild directive, pulsing exaggerated life into every particle of oxygen holding us together.

His eyes widened, and fat Jonny jumped higher than a frog on a skillet looking for his legs.

Running from the oleanders toward the hooligans ahead. Gone forever, leaving my lust for adventure in his dust, with the first taste of shame of what I'd proffered lingering on my lips.

Alone, in the still scent of the cool soft oleanders of summer I breathed their silence of innocence goodbye, forever folding the sweet smell of sin in the shadow of my scarlet desire.

Utility

By Gigi Benson

Sitting on the cool cement of the utility closet she listened, waiting for the swoosh of her mother's thighs wrapped in navy blue polyester. One hand cupped tight on her little brother Matt's mouth, her other loosened as the heavy varicose veins moved across the grate, holding her breath in his, their molecules suspended, then swirled as the swishing stood still, the thighs had arrived, they turned in front, then sideways, they were thinking while inside she and Matthew held their breath, panic starting to rise inside her.

What if her mother saw her fingers curled around the wires of the grate?

She couldn't move them.

They would be discovered.

Could she push Matt behind her — the boiler wasn't on. She stared at her mother's thighs. Could they make a run for it through those pillars and down the hall?

She longed for the hallway, the runway to freedom.

Down, past the bedrooms, cut through the den and across to the dining room.

Front door or go for the kitchen?

No, no, too many utensils, wooden spoons, plates that break, her mind raced, yes better to go through the front door and out to the street where neighbors could see. Safety.

Slowly, silently, she lifted her fingers up, then back and out from the grate.

MOVE, she willed, "Move Away Mom," she begged the atoms to rearrange themselves.

Science teacher Mr. Casey had said they could, yes, the atoms were moving all the time, it was actually possible, a physical possibility if one could only time it right — he showed how a hand could go through matter.

If she could only know, find that moment. And escape to the other side of the wall.

But then Matthew would be left alone, he'd cry out, Mom would open the door and discover them, revealing their hiding place.

Heavy regret consumed her: Why did she pull him in with her anyway? Mom never hurt Matt, he was her favorite, Mom wouldn't hit him, no, Mom would run after her.

Cursing herself for momentary weakness, how could she even think of abandoning him?

She loosened her hand against his mouth as the swoosh moved down the hallway.

They clung to each other in relief. They were safe. Safe, listening in unison as the atoms gave way for them to move, through the door, and down the hallway, to disappear.

Water Broke

By Gigi Benson

Thinking of my mom some 45 years ago trying to put the charcoal filter together for brother Marky's 8th birthday aquarium while breathing through labor pains and instructing me how to make split pea soup with ham hocks.

When her water broke and Dad still wasn't home, I was sorely missing Ellen who had run the house since she was six. She'd been packed off to St. Scholastica's nuns for a "better education than our high schools could provide." At least that's what mom and dad said. (We knew it was really to get her the hell out of Arizona and the "sock it to 'em" '70s.)

Eddie was off at Uncle Ed's military camp, and Bobby had gone running up the street to ask Dr. Christensen to come help. Mom screamed after him, "Ask Marie for some candles — eight, we just need eight candles."

So here I was at 12 years old faced with birthing a baby right there in our kitchen.

I poured water into the fish tank and whacked at the ham hocks. I tried to remember what Prissy did when Miss Scarlett started having her baby. I filled the biggest pot we had with water and put it on the stove to heat. I didn't know how

13

that water got used but I thought that's what Mammy would say to do.

Bobby came back at some point (without the doctor), and we put the eight fish that were squirming in the baggy into the tank, then helped my mom lie down on the floor while she panted through icing the cake on the step stool. Mom's favorite, Matt, climbed up the table and put the hose on the filter, plugged it in and it started to burble while Tricia snuck an Orange Crush from the fridge. It would be her last day as the youngest so she was rooting for it.

At some point during all this the doctor's wife, Mrs. Christensen, came in (with the eight candles), took one look at the situation and told Mom to get in her car. But Mom wouldn't budge till we sang happy birthday — which we did as if we were at a pizza parlor — and then I was left alone wiping up goopy water that most definitely was not from the fish tank while Marky ate away at his lopsided German chocolate cake off one of the blue and white *Happy Birthday 8 Years Old!* plates with matching napkins Mom had bought for the occasion.

Dad drove up, told me to get Mom's "hurry bag" and scooped Mom out of Mrs. Christensen's car and into his. Moved by the excitement, Mrs. Christensen uncharacteristically offered her backyard to host the birthday party. They had a pool that was way more exciting than a new baby, and we all promptly stripped down and suited up to jump in.

Mom came home a couple of days later, with a pink Mary Bridget for all of us to adore. It was a happy, happy time in a crazy chaotic world … I felt she was the most delicate thing I'd ever seen, making everyone quiet and sweet and still. For a bit.

Novel Mortality

By Gigi Benson

When I was in fourth grade my mother was rereading *Of Human Bondage*. She read voraciously, every night after we were "put away," which meant in our rooms and under the covers like letters in an envelope waiting on the foyer table to be mailed in the next morning's post.

With our Dad out selling life insurance, a load of wash on the spin cycle meant she was deep in another world and we were free to roam, whether that meant slipping out the window to meet up with best friends under Mrs. Crosby's carport or sneaking around to the kitchen to steal some sugary cereal. If it was a weekend, sleepovers were in process, which meant numerous trips to the bathroom to bring back toilet paper, pajamas over our runaway clothes, and grabbing a few forks from the kitchen to arm ourselves as we went into the desert night to TP someone's front yard. Mom blissfully feigned ignorance, only too happy to have us out decorating someone's yard instead of making a mess in her kitchen.

Escaping into a novel was my mother's only sure bet to be alone, reading two or three books a week. Reflecting on this I now realize that 1) She most assuredly was sleep deprived, and

2) The novels became the only world where she didn't hear other voices than the author's. In her schizophrenic mind the book became life and life became the book. She counted on the writer taking her away from the present, which too often presented confrontation, structure and abandonment.

Having eight children kept her mind preoccupied, but when we were finally asleep she often went mad in the quiet. This made our life surreal, and until we each left home we didn't really know what reality was as a single individual.

She once told me reading had taught her that "Mortality is based on the understanding one is alive, that there is something to live for." This understanding my mother had in psychotic spades. She had survived epic emotions, starting with her own inconvenient birth on Black Tuesday of the Great Depression. She had a thyroid condition which almost killed her more times than she had failed at killing herself.

However, when my mother threw my cat out of a speeding car for climbing her favorite curtains, it left an indelible impression of the power an adult holds over life, and the wide range of value they hold on life itself.

KittyClump was the offspring of my older sister's cat Cassandra, a majestic long-haired calico that my mother adored. Unfortunately she bore no resemblance to her mother, with extra claws on every paw so when she walked across the floor you'd hear her clip-clap claws coming. Obviously she wasn't a mouser.

I loved her all the more for this wacky clumpy deformity. She wasn't beautiful — a fur ball with a big white spot on her little black nose, she looked like a cartoon drawing. Unlike the deft darling diva Cassandra who maneuvered effortlessly between Mom's vases on the piano once we'd all been bundled off to bed, KittyClump lumbered along like a bottom feeder beneath Cassandra's aerial antics.

Until she discovered the drapes. The drapes were her undoing. My mom relished the dramatic drapes adorning and framing the huge endless windows throughout our new ranch house. They were grand, theatrical, and KittyClump waited in the wings to take stage!

I was in the hallway when I heard the scream; amazed, I turned to see my mom leap across the table full force, shoes still on. I ran in horror toward my screaming mom as she lunged up the curtains, and grabbed KittyClump by the neck, falling alongside curtain rods, swinging chandelier lights and her precious high back chairs in a crescendo of chaos. She held the screeching cat high above her shoulder, shaking her as she grabbed her keys from the hook, kicked open the kitchen door and disappeared into the carport. I could hear our Oldsmobile 98 door slam. With anger in her engine and high pitch howling she roared away down the domicile dotted cul de sac of sensible sleeping children tucked into bed.

I waited.

She came back a couple hours later. I waited at the end of my bed. She told my sister to put the little kids to bed and sat down next to me.

I asked her where my cat was.

She said, "In a better place than here."

I was fighting the wet snot gathering in my nose, not taking my eyes off her, and in a low, measured voice I demanded, "Where? Where is she?"

She pulled out a little silver pen, shining in a smooth satin-lined black box.

She had put the top of the box on the bottom for presentation, a deep sapphire blue silk holding it to catch the light.

"Look, it lights up" she said, lifting it out of the box as if it was a jewel.

She clicked the light on, "You can write in the dark even." She aimed it at the ceiling making curlicue circles above us.

"Your dad won it at the blackjack tournament!"

"See," she turned it and you could read *The Sands* in big loopy cursive characters.

I looked straight up into her eyes, and in the measured steady voice of a woman far older than I, said, "I want my cat, not your stupid pen."

She balked. I didn't know if she was going to slap me or scream.

Instead she rushed from the room, down the hall and slammed her door behind her. We heard the door lock flip, and breathed.

No one talked about KittyClump, and when my dad came home no one mentioned the cat. Like the Sugar Smacks the night after shopping day, the cat was gone.

However, when she showed up six weeks later scratching at our bedroom window in the rain Mom had a newfound respect for that cat.

"I'll be damned, she should be dead."

I followed her into her room, intent on finding out why she had lied to me.

She had gone into the bathroom, her book *Of Human Bondage* lying on her bed stand. It looked formidable. I took it.

I started reading it secretly and disappeared into her mind, a warped attempt to be inside her, knowing a private world none of my seven siblings could compete with. I would hide it in between my mattress or up in the tree fort wrapped in my old coat when I had to leave the house.

I skipped school for the first time in my life, nestling like my personal heroine Scarlett O'Hara under the huge cottonwoods planted some decades before to shade the open irrigation canals running for miles along Central Avenue.

I disappeared into my mother's world, twisted lives of trauma and mayhem abounding, sorrow so deep and profound there was no cure.

I learned my mother's delicious secret of living beyond oneself, a voyeur peeking through a strange crack into her unnerving grip on faith, and a wry wisdom never witnessed in our waking hours. For years I continued to violate her privacy by sneaking into her room and reading whatever book she was immersed in.

I felt a keen power knowing what world she was escaping into. I knew her, secretly traveling the same adventure — I alone knew where she was in her adventure, albeit a page or two behind.

Years later my mom visited me after I'd had my second son. I was sitting alone in my room after a postpartum tantrum that would have rivaled one of her hysterical fits, and she came in to coax me out of the shame she knew so well. When she sat down next to me she saw it on my shelf.

"Oh I loved that book, read it two or three times," she said.

"I stole it from you." I admitted to my shame.

"What?"

19

"When you took KittyClump away."

"Oh my lord, that cat. She shouldn't have lived, I must have been going 70 miles an hour when I threw her out the window."

She looked down at the book. "Well, that's a story that you can use somewhere — this book would never have been written if Somerset Maugham had had an easy life."

"Mom, the SPCA might come after you if I write about that," I said.

"Nonsense, I've already been locked up, and as he said himself when his family got upset about the story, it was a novel, not an autobiography."

Curious, I looked up his quote: 'This is a novel, not an autobiography; though much in it is autobiographical, more is pure invention.'

For me, my mother and all those who travel the orphan's journey, it offers strange comfort that we are not alone. Here or in the hereafter of invention.

One page at a time.

Dead Wit

By Gigi Benson

I've been dead twice — once only briefly and a second time
long enough to have welts on my budding breasts from those
paddles that sideline the flatline back.

Both times I got a glimpse of heaven, and it taught me
there's every possibility to traverse from mortal meanderings
to the temporal lodgings of infinity. The first time was too
early to recall vividly, being smacked down by a semi truck as I
crossed what I thought was a green light — parents, teach
your seven year olds which green light matters at an
intersection!

Luckily the truck was so high off the ground it barely
grazed me, although it knocked me unconscious.

For one short instant I left my body to survive, watching
white coats come and go from a third eye till I woke up three
days later with my then six siblings ready to raise a ruckus,
brain injury or not.

Of course, brief as that was, the big one was when I was
welded between the two bucket seats of a Karmann Ghia with
four other teenagers' guts and bones crackling from a 1970
Lincoln Continental crammed up our Volkswagen's ventilators,

repositioned to the back jumpseat. My older brother Bobby bowed about the bent and blaring steering wheel and big Barbara hanging halfway out the dangling door. I was squished between her twitching calves in the well of what had been the passenger seat shared moments before.

Only Bobby saw it, "like lightning" he'd say in court, the station wagon in front of us with two kids bouncing in the back flying sideways as their mom swerved, the car to our right squealing brakes as it veered to the left, then a sheet of shining chrome jumping over the median between two Phoenician palms — headlights flying as we spun out along McDonald Drive through the the infamous red buttes of square peak's bosom.

Bobby tried to control the car, gripping so hard on the steering wheel it welded in his scrawny 17-year-old hands from a circle to a rectangle upon impact. (This odd piece of detail we learned when the wheel was presented as Exhibit 12B at the trial where Barbara got a shit load settlement for splattering her spleen across the street.)

That trial, and my own subsequent one, turned into an unintended reality lesson of the mechanics of getting into heaven via metal objects aiding and abetting one there. In motor vehicle accidents folks don't get there upon impact: First your body flies forward, smacks on the dashboard — or whatever is in front of it (if another passenger isn't sitting on your lap), whereupon you fall back, really helping those concussion clots colluding at the back of your brain, and only then do you fly forward again through the windshield.

So we hit the back of those groovy new-fangled headrests, and since I was sitting in between the bucket seats I fell sideways across Big Barbara, pressing her against the door latch and instantaneously releasing it to send her and her spleen to the side, inadvertently providing a limp for life … but a life all the same. My head had hit the glove compartment and when her huge mass went out I went down into the well where parts of Herb Leib's front bumper rested with my mashed mush for the medics to maneuver.

Our ingenious German engine was in the back so the three teens above could have blown up but it had conveniently popped out the back of the car and lay innocently under a street lamp a good 60 yards behind us. But Heaven, oh sweet heaven, loomed before us.

I was watching the engine parts roll above and fly backwards over us, a warm and soft and tingling feeling filling me, no fear, no pain, just joy at the quiet roaring bringing me backwards and away from Earth.

There were no sirens. Silence sweeter than any sound of a seashell's song cradled my release from the earthly realm while whirling molecules drifted from connected cells, congealing epidermis into winsome wisps unweaving in wonder whilst kinetic energies bonded the body together and buoyed me away from Earth's gravity, gaining speed as the starlights shimmered, soaring between the mortal matter's pull. Heaven held me safe, if only for a moment, saving my Milky Way matter for another go on the planet.

I took it.

The Sky's the Limit

By Gigi Benson

This is the sentence I waited for.

Only I didn't want Fred Astaire to say it, too erudite for me.

No, Clark Gable. Rhett Butler.

I think I heard it first from my Dad, when we'd bustle into a booth and the waitress would look forlorn fearing we'd all order the kid's 99-cent special. He'd endear himself to her and ourselves by loudly pronouncing our favorite feeling-fun-forever line.

"The sky's the limit."

One night not in July I heard firecrackers going off.

I rose and went to the back hallway door where you could see the whole sky falling down to the Arizona desert orange groves surrounding our house, amazing sky torpedos blasting beyond the dark blanket of babies. The whole house woke and soon enough Dad himself opened the door so we could filter out, standing in silence — all seven of us and him.

He whistled his navy whistle, long and low leaning into the night.

"The sky's the limit."

We silently followed him through the back door and into the kitchen where he scrambled up some midnight eggs and bacon. We ate them in the cool 102-degree 1:34 a.m. air with every door and window in the house open. Even the front door.

No one talked or we woulda woke up Mom.

It was like a secret sect indulging in ketchup on warmed-up tater tots and big slabs of bacon only Dad knew how to make Chicago-style.

Tricia had fallen back asleep so I lifted her up with Marky and we sleepwalked her down the hall to her bed.

We didn't brush our teeth.

Ellen and Bobby did the dishes and then Dad turned out the light.

One more whistle as he closed the front door behind him.

We'd skipped his light fantastic in a barren sky that had no bounds.

He was our hero.

WoHeLo

By Gigi Benson

Sing Wo He Lo
Sing Wo He Lo
Work, Health and Love.

I never quite remember the actual lyrics to our Camp Fire Girls chant, though the first and the last three words still often come to me in the middle of a task. "Work, Health and Love" had been revamped from whatever Native American words had really been uttered for female virtues sustaining their existence. Perhaps two out of three were whispered arduously out there in their soon to be lost land.

That said, I was ignorantly game for Camp Fire Girls (Girl Scout light with a Catholic flair), my mother's sole step into the well-intentioned "Indian lore." I'm sure her intention was to embrace the *Diné,* or "The People," to honor the teensy sliver of Cherokee blood supposedly running through our veins from her mad Missouri ancestors.

And no question they were crazy. One summer in Springfield, Illinois, with Daddy Joe and you knew you had "Injun blood." I liked the idea I had something foreign running through my veins, beyond the rebel Scotch Irish, something that tied me to this land, another people.

Our brown and tan felt robes were a sad homage to those fierce warriors. I particularly liked the odd stomping dances and howling. I cringe in what should be shame at the delight we had crying out and shaking our arms to the Sun God in what had to be the best "Gunsmoke" send-up ever done on the Sun Dance.

I tip my hat to my mom though on her commitment to making the most of developing our characters and exposing us to the culture we'd landed in due to a fan belt breaking before she and my dad could get us to California. With four kids and no money he got a job from the gas station selling U-Test-M tube machines and there we were in "Fonix" for the rest of our lives. Well, for a long part of them anyway.

It wasn't until years later when I went to care for her after a stroke that my mom admitted her ignorance and misplaced ardor far beyond the worst silver screen representations of "tamed natives." She whispered as if we were in a confessional, trying to make sense of the failure to bring the cultures together through the "Mother's Helpers" program where young teens were ripped from their reservations and sent to the now infamous "Phoenix Indian School" throughout the '60s.

"We just wanted to save them," she said.

"From what?" I asked.

"From us."

We both hung our heads at the reality that we'd been a part of a great wrongdoing, and one that was perhaps still happening.

I was stunned at her clarity — especially given she had stepped well into dementia after several cerebral strokes — as she recalled the whole debacle and her ignorance of what they were doing. She was horrified at the decades late realization that her "hosting" girls from the Indian School implicated us.

"They were basically stolen from their families, farmed out as free nannies."

As she spoke I was reminded of how regal, stunning really, she could be when she led us in our chants. A momentary transformation from the bat-ass crazy mother to a regal elder from a bygone time when air brought messages on the winds warning wise women of imminent dangers only the strongest seers could see.

"I was trying to help," she said to herself, and closed her eyes against the memory.

Then, with a characteristic schizophrenic switch her voice became hardened, "I needed help."

I almost said something, maybe reminding her how she'd helped Loretta get a job after she graduated, or how Dad had taught her to drive. Then I remembered Maya, who'd stolen Mom's jewelry, and thought to start going through the different summers would be dangerous and only make it worse. Loretta had really loved us though, hadn't she? She was so much fun, she took us up on the roof, she wasn't afraid of anything. I had loved Loretta. She saved us from Mom.

The dropped left side of her face twitched from the effort to speak succinctly. "I'll burn in hell for it," she whispered.

And then she was back. But quiet.

Reflecting as I recall this, I realize it was one of the few private moments of admiration I had with my mother, poignantly reminding me of her rarely seen power to rise above the mantle of shame masking her manic mind, to be lucid.

She would hold stage in the middle of our makeshift carport cleared for the meeting, with one arm raised to the sun, a single arrow in her fist, her eyes wide, lifting us to the eternally empty Maricopa skies.

A blue so vast we lost ourselves in hope.

Predator's Point of View

By Gigi Benson

In the dark one naturally is attracted to shiny, iridescent objects.

The deeper the indigo element of one's soul, the greater the appreciation of rising to the top, skimming the tip-top waves of innocence, delighting in the simple sprays of spring shooting across the sky as one comes up for air.

Sucking in the sweet smells sailing on across one's senses.

It is the smell that dooms me.

Try as I might, I cannot resist.

All the baubles and babbling can be ignored, but the scent of hope, of change, of newness undoes me.

Any resolve to restrain myself disappears and I sink into a delicious state of euphoria, my mind racing, climbing through the hexagrams before me, psychically capable of measuring the distance, depth, diameter of my prey.

I can taste it in the back of my gums. But the most delicious is smelling the pores of my selected morsel getting stronger as I advance.

If it moves, I move.
If it breathes, I inhale.
Deep down into my deepest belly.
If it turns, its eyes locking with mine
I swallow.

Insect ingested.

Débuts Avant de Commencer

By Gigi Benson

"Qu'est que tu veux?"

I lay against the bed on the floor, like a child-doll spent from play, the sheets still cupping me in their sweet sweat as the morning air held each particle aloft in time. I brushed my hair away from my forehead and smelled the strange mix of lovemaking with blood against my cheek, staring down between my legs, surprised and curious alone with his mark on me forever.

Hours before we'd arrived, we had shuttled across the train tracks together through the Alps, and got waylaid in Nice, only to finally find Aix-en-Provence shuttered in the witching hour. We'd kept each other entertained, the only two Americans on board who knew Jimmy Carter was more than a peanut president, delighting in the camaraderie of spring break abroad, sharing stories as strangers do when there's no reason not to when a four-hour train ride turns into 20.

He was on his way to an internship in Nice, his last step before residency in NYC. I was escaping from my bickering French family hosts before heading off to audition at the

Royal Academy of Dramatic Art in London for a Shakespeare Study Scholarship that would lead to an MFA.

I assumed a preposterous woman of the world worthy of a Merchant Ivory film jaw and spoke of my lover pining for me back in the flatirons of Boulder, while he revealed his dashed hopes with a pre-med romance never meant to be and the recent, rash decision to run off to France for the summer only a fortnight before.

We laughed at the penniless plight of our adventures and traded tips we'd learned for the destinations we were tunneling toward, glad to speak in the foreign language of *American Anglaise* we were sure none of our fellow passengers understood.

We were equally impressed with each other which made the conversation all the more titillating since we would probably never meet again once I disembarked the train.

Oh so we thought.

The train was delayed for four hours en route. "*Que-est que tu veux?*" he asked in his best Cleveland French accent as he bounded off the train. "Surprise me," I quipped.

He brought me back a lemon ice and I counted my francs to repay him, which he dutifully refused. I insisted, "You're not a doctor yet and we're both broker than we should be on a trip like this!" He pocketed it and blushed.

We sat in a queer comforting silence imprisoned in the light dabbling through the overhead glass turning everything a soft golden glow as the sun set and we wondered what French words to use to ask when, if ever, we would resume our travels.

Pulling into the next station they announced it would be held until morning. There was no station to sit in, just rows of uninviting wrought iron benches. The porter pointed up the hill to the lone hotel as he hopped back onto the back of the train. *"Bon Nuit!"*

The somber concierge was not amused at our gaiety entering past midnight, mumbling, *"Qu'est-ce que vous voulez?"*

"Two, *deux chambres s'il vous plait,"* I replied.

"Il n'y a qu'une seule chambre disponible," he responded.

"Une seule *chambre?"* I said, surprised.

The soon to be a doctor took both our bags, one in each hand, *"Que-est que tu veux?* We'll save money … *ça va?"*

"D'accord," I agreed, grabbing my bag out of his hand and hiking up the stairs as if we were on a Camp Fire Girl adventure. I was glad to be saving on the unexpected expense and fully intended to flip a coin for the couch.

When we opened the door I was surprised how small the room was, just big enough for the one double bed. Where was the little French *pièce d'résistance* Lillie Langtry would lounge on?

We looked at each other.

"Well at least we're not camping on the benches," he said.

I acted like it was no big deal, we were camping indoors.

"Que-est que tu veux?" I asked, indicating the bed or the floor.

He turned off the light, dropped his pants and got into the bed. "Sleep."

I turned to the mustard plaster wall, bathed in a chill blue light from the wide open window slats.

"Quelle surprise," I muttered at the maleness of it all.

I took off my first layer of clothing wondering where my exhibitionist tendencies had gone when I needed them. I pulled the slats closed and slipped between the sheets with my "child's armor" still intact.

35

Amazing how a good cross-your-heart bra and panties (with the days of the week on them) can make you feel fully clothed while horizontal in the dark with a semi stranger you've shared your deepest secrets with all day.

I breathed in the dark indigo air now turning sapphire as night settled in through the slats.

"*Que-est que tu veux?*" he asked.

He sounded kind, vulnerable, honest.

I opened my mouth, and a bawdy Belle Starr laugh filled the room.

"You surprise me," he said as if speaking to the ceiling.

"*Et vous,*" I replied. Edith Piaf seemed to be entering my body. It was heady.

"Is this ok?" he asked.

I couldn't remember the French word for camping, so I just said, "*Que-est que tu veux?*"

"*Les lune,*" he said to the ceiling.

The moon had just moved across the window, lighting the sheet across us like a tent.

"*La lune,*" I corrected.

We laughed.

I woke to him beside me, the sun rising, and he reached over, outlining my cheekbone with his soon to be a surgeon's finger, around my ear, down my neck and then pulling me on top of him. Again.

Showered and clean, he stood in front of the window, hands on hips like a gendarme recruit ready to report. "I might make the next train — meet you downstairs for coffee if I miss it?" I smiled like the sphinx, pulled the sheets around me and turned away as he lumbered down the stairs.

I slipped down the side of the bed. My mind racing, a wave of relief washed over me as I thanked my stars for the inconvenient blessed birth control blood. I hadn't had a period in months. It was an awful lot of blood for a period. Whatever it was, it had stopped. Then I turned red as the crimson stripes across the sheets, wondering if the blood had gotten on him. Is that why he showered? Why he had left so suddenly?

Try as I might, I could not be embarrassed. Sighing into myself I rolled across the floor, landing flat against the bed's sideboard, soaking in the sunlight searing through the window like a stage set just waiting to be played upon. I lay naked in my own body, full and ripe and ravaged. All nineteen and a half years met with the simplest of acts in the dead of night. I felt no remorse, no betrayal for my forgotten love a continent away. Alone now, quiet and blissfully bled.

I reveled in the moment and touched the soft fleshy fold of my thigh, watching the blood slide down to my calf until it ran clear just above my ankle.

"J'arrive."

Chinook

By Gigi Benson

She did not know how it would be done, or that she would be the one to do it, but only that it must be done. Turn. Him. Over.

She pushed her heavy coat sleeves up as high as she could and slipped her arms under the soft belly facing her, blood glistening against the winter moon which guided her to the ribs. She could feel one was broken, and pushed her hands down into the hard ice earth afraid she might tear his insides if she rolled too quickly.

Voices were calling out from down the road, she could not answer. Her body had become one with this broken being, much bigger but younger than her.

She put her lips to his and felt a short shallow breath, brief but there.

He was with her.

With her free arm she reached down to feel his hips — the legs did not make sense. His pants were half on, his back shredded with gravel. She felt the highway grit embedded in his skin sticking out from the jeans above his thigh. She leaned back and the lone streetlight caught the jagged bone protruding from his shin. She started to choke, vomit rising in her throat. She swallowed it, cupping his stomach as it heaved and he started to curl up. She knew she just had to hold him, keep his extending stomach in one place, wishing someone would come and help hold him together. She thought she was supposed to compress something, what was she supposed to compress? He started to shake so she pulled him closer, getting her chin onto his neck and over his shoulder so she had their weight in control, wrapping him tight, like she was a human tourniquet.

He stopped shaking. She looked out across the road, up the hill where the truck that had dragged him must have gone. She wouldn't know for years why the Wyoming night was so still, the winter sky stood in shame for witnessing such wrongdoing.

She heard the siren, then her friends calling out to the police, to "go up the hill."

The snow was too deep so the patrol car skidded. She jumped, afraid they wouldn't see them smack dab in the middle of the road, his bones rattling against her ribs. He'd peed all over her.

She saw the lights hitting the treetops, pulling the sound from the bottom of her belly so she didn't move him, she called across the warm dry wind rolling down the mountain.

"Here. We are here," she called.

No sound came back, just the long, low chinook, rolling silently up to them across the moon-struck prairie.

Years later, shivering in an off-Broadway theater, far from the Vedauwoo world of Wyoming she smelled him, his thin breath rising inside her clavicles, while the story of another boy from the equal rights state unraveled on the stage below her. Perhaps it was the dark, and the relation of the stage to her last-row seat high in back that brought the wilds of Wyoming back in her lap. Or the position of the stage down low, her seat up high, the lighting similar, but no, it was the dark, the weird warm with a layer of cold, yes, the shadows were the same.

But this boy onstage who was whipped and hung on a barbed wire fence left to die, this boy had a name, Matthew Shepard. Her boy remained nameless. He was from Laramie, way south of this Sheridan boy. Or was it Casper? She'd forgotten. She was confused, her eyes were on the stage but her body was wrapped in a bloody parka from a decade before, dancing between the actors' lines and the weird warm winds of Wyoming, watching an ambulance load him in the dark from the roadside.

The sheriff had reached out his gnarly leather glove to her, thanking her "for your troubles" and told her to "head back down the road" to join her group. "They're waiting for ya, we're done here. Best you get back down the road now."

But she was still holding him to her, shaking in rhythm to his shivering stupor.

There was no one to take him. Did someone take him?

Yes, the sirens, they weren't on stage, were there sirens? Or did they carry him into their car?

The actors on stage were talking, but the sheriff's voice was in her head.

"Go on now, we'll git him fixed up, we take care of our own, so don't you worry 'bout him."

Someone on stage moved a chair, but she heard their boots crunching into the snow, flashlights darting across their bodies as the men lifted him off her, she screamed, "his guts," her hands reaching to catch them, but only a weird white plasma drizzled onto her palms.

They wiped him off her, yes, two of them, deputies? They had coarse blue paper towels, like the ones they use in a car wash.

She watched as they rolled him into a sheet, no, it must have been a stretcher. She hoped it was a stretcher. If there was a stretcher there must have been an ambulance. But she didn't remember sirens, and no red light, just the headlights, showing the track marks of the truck. His pants pulled down to his ankles, black grit embedded in his thighs scratching against her. Or was that in the play?

"You need help going down?" the sheriff asked.

The lights went out, leaving only the shadow of barbed wire across the stage.

The audience gasped.

She shook her head, remembered rolling over, and how when the men took him off her, he cried out.

It was the only cry she heard.

Freesia

By Gigi Benson

He stood behind the pillar, watching her deplane, holding onto the freesia, fragrant and frivolous among the wilting lilies, his hand clasped about their wrapping, the card slipping from his grip.

He turned, bending down carefully not to crush them, reaching instinctively under the classic chrome frame and past the black leathered Barcelona square airport lounger cushion, when a soft baritone hand touched his.

"Did you lose this?" the brown eyes falling down upon him queried.

He stammered, blood rising to his temples, dizzy with the thrill of the touch, the voice, the secret intimacy so quickly shared.

"Oh, thank you, yes, it's ...

"For your sweetheart," the handsome chin intoned, finishing his sentence.

She spun around the pillar, arms open, her green sapphire spheres spinning down to see their hands, still entwined, no breath left between the trio in this slice of a second hanging betwixt them.

Yule Tide Turn

By Gigi Benson

You.
Sitting in the high back corner chair I bought so many years
ago I can't remember,
save that it was for you,
as my feet still don't touch the ground.
Yours did though,
For a very long time.

A time that seems story book now,
All the rough edges rounded
Softened
Sad
In their winsome not to be thought about too often state
Threadbare like the chair
That you sat in for the first time in 20 some years
on a visit to my home
Not yours
With our sons
It still fit you.
With the footstool you had bought for me pushed aside,

since I was not in my seat.
My guest was.
In the seat that is. Of the chair.
You were my guest.
Comfortable, in the corner pocket,
surprised you fit.
I remembered, later, not at the time, but later
How when we met you said you always felt odd,
Like you didn't fit
Then I remembered us in Nederland,
For a fleeting moment,
In a makeshift cabin above the treeline,
a cast iron stove and a blanket of down parkas to keep us
warm, discovering each strange feeling inside each other,
exhilarated and exhausted, the Colorado winter whirling white
wisps of magic, we lay watching,
warm limbs entwined like lace,
our breath still, frozen awe held in the odd light of dusk
descending,
Quiet streams of gold slipping through the blue spruce in
silence.
How afterwards — on the way down the canyon —
you said you felt you rarely fit.
Like a jigsaw, a piece of a puzzle, but ...
"We fit."
I was so pleased to fit.
Particularly for someone who felt they never fit.
And now our boys fit.
So happy
To be gathered under one roof

Pecan pie waiting in the other room.
But for a moment,
We are together in seats we use to know.
With new bottoms, a bit softer, skinnier, padding our getting old bones
In new lives.
Sitting.
Without rancor, without regret, sharing our sons' lives as parents.
Two decades of dissent mellowed in the Christmas moment,
For the children,
Two grown men
An unexpected gift.
These two wonderful humans we made,
Making us human,
Once again
In peace.

The Only Sound in the Room

By Gigi Benson

I go to the woods to hear the quiet breathing, still.
It does not haunt me, but it waits.
Like a cat.
Green emerald eyes at the end of the hall
Deep eyes seeing beyond, through you.
Waiting — no — observing — all the while taking it in
Empowering its instinctive prowess manifold
Just by being still.
Unnerving the object of its affection
Unmoved by the emotional life of a mere human
Every so often piercing its veil of objectivity by sharing its
sorrow,
Or extending its compassion for yours.
If it's particularly invested it will close its eyes and open them
Acknowledging you've shared your inner soul and been heard
— Or recognized,
Felt.
It's a dangerous feat for a non-human
And probably why the Egyptians honored them,
Revered them, preferred them.

What secrets did they witness?

If one steps back and considers all the arcane mortal antics animals witness it is staggering.

Think about it.

Some of the scenes between battling spouses could determine child custody cases.

Now dogs might show favoritism, and parakeets — just forget it, and gerbils, no, they could not reliably recall the facts.

But a cat, yes. A cat would be a formidable judge jockeying the Heavens and the Heaven-Nots.

But seriously, I do wonder in the wee hours of dark night what my cat might do were I to fall to felony?

Would he back me up?

Understanding why I thrust the knife through my lover's side, slitting the spleen and retching back in horror as the blade flew across the floor?

The cat lifts his leg and movs it to one side, staring at the blood.

He leans down to smell it, sensing the sharp edge and delicately laying his tongue flat across the top of the blade to taste the rich red ribbon of his mistress's fatal folly.

Numb — I sink into his eyes.

No judgment.

He waits.

Unlike the spattered lover lying, twitching, on the floor in spasms

His eyes are clenched,

His fists grinding, grasping his own knuckles

Rubbing them raw as he reaches out

His eyeballs rolling inside their sockets

His mouth sucking in gasps of quiet air,

The only sound in the room.
And the cat walks through it
to the other side of sanity.

Dan Eeds

Missadelphia - 1961

By Dan Eeds

We're new to Missadelphia. Mama says it takes seven years to win over small-town folk. How small is small? The mayor — Mayor Riggs — serves as school board president and is co-founder of the White Citizens' Council — an active civic organization comprised of a banker, two ministers, a vice-principal and other men of high community standing.

Papa has just finished his first year teaching band at Missadelphia's General Patrick Cleburne High School. Mama claims kinship to the general who'd advocated for the emancipation of the slaves so's they could join our southern cause. Mama says the general was a visionary. Papa says it was a miracle that it was a Yankee and not Johnny Reb that laid the general in his grave.

Enough ancient history. I'm Leigh. I'm nearly 12.

Braving the day's swelter, I traverse the city on a mission of grave importance. Looking both ways, I cross the highway coming from Meridian, hurry past the Auto Wreckers' Emporium, and stop dead in my tracks. I read the fresh stenciling on Mayor Riggs' Super Service restroom door,

Ladies
No Coons Allowed

The black paint is glossy-wet, still drying.

"Hey, Baby Girl," my father calls out through the open door. Today, he's busy doing his summer job pumping gas for Mayor Riggs. But he'd hand-on-heart promised to stop calling me "Baby Girl."

"Baby Girl, you look like a piece of wilted lettuce. Come inside and see my new office." He's hunched over a desk-top office machine, studying its matrix of buttons. "Watch this." He pushes a button, and the machine jumps to life with a cacophony of whirring gears, and after several seconds goes, "clunk."

"See that?" he says proudly, "One-hundred fifty dollars, and twelve cents."

"I can add faster than that hunk of metal."

He frowns and pouts a lip.

"Papa, you're looking sharp in that gas station uniform."

"You like it better than my teacher's uniform?"

"The hat makes you look like an admiral or maybe even a sergeant." Truth be told, I'm not fond of his teacher's uniform: white short-sleeve shirt with ink stains and clip-on bowtie, askew. I'll stop there, except to mention how much I'm fretting about the day I turn 14 and walk through the doors of Patrick Cleburne High with Papa's greeting shoutout. "Hey, Baby Girl, welcome to the ninth grade!" It's a terrifying scenario — a dark cloud hanging over my future.

"Papa, I need to tell you something important. But first, I'm dying for one of your ice-cold Dr Peppers."

"They are Mayor Riggs' Dr Peppers. Everyone pays, even my Little Miss 10, 2 and 4."

Now it's Little Miss?! "The mayor doesn't even know me."

"And that's his loss. So how's your summer vacation been so far?"

"Stressful."

The telephone rings.

"Hold on, Leigh." Bright as a TV weatherman, he says into the phone, "Mayor's Super Service! ... Oh, Mayor Riggs, it's you again." He nods, "Yes sir, the new signs are up. Hold on, Mayor." He cradles the receiver atop his shoulder, digs into a pocket, and flips me a dime. "Go," he says, pointing to the QuikKold machine next to the lube pit.

A minute later, strolling back from the soda machine, I duck down and creep stealthily forward. Through the doorway, I hear Papa saying, "We already had the 'Whites Only' signs, guess that wasn't polite enough."

The Mayor's muffled squawking is coming through the phone.

Papa says, "To tell the truth, the new signs are an embarrassment."

I move closer. This is getting interesting. I scuttle low through the open door and squeeze into a niche at the front of the metal desk. Now I can almost hear the Mayor's end of the conversation. I pop my head up and rest my chin atop the desk. Seeing my bodiless head, he spins away in his swivel chair, pulling the phone cord over his shoulder. Sneaky-like, I come around the desk and press my ear directly into the receiver, alongside his ear.

He nearly drops the phone and gives me a pinched expression. But now I'm hearing the Mayor clear as day, saying, "Galen, it takes time for a new family to feel part of our community. Missadelphians are different from y'all cosmopolitans up in Little Rock. I suggest y'all familiarize and show some fortitude."

"It's vulgar."

"Now hold on, Galen. Don't worry yourself, it ain't for our town folk, they knows what's what. It's for those unfamiliar with our community." The mayor's voice is coming through louder and clearer. "It's only temporary till this hullabaloo blows over. As mayor, it's my job to protect the sanctity of this community. Here's my message, 'FREEDOM RIDERS, GO HOME.' Y'all know Wilcox? Chairs the local necktie committee?"

Papa's back stiffens and he shoots me a weird twitchy look. "You're telling me this Wilcox fella is a klansman?"

"All I'm sayin', it's not happening on my watch. Wilcox tells me, and I'm quoting, 'Me and my boys have an action-packed surprise for them Freedom Riders.' The man's a psychopath. *Oh*, by the way, Galen, I'm coming by the Super Service at five so's you can wash the El Dorado. Also, I wanted to congratulate you and your high school Rebels for their victory at the State Band Championship. Y'all put my town on the map."

Papa hangs up and smiles at me rolling an icy bottle of Dr Pepper across my forehead.

"Let's start again," he says, "How's your day been?"

"My new friend Dwight says, 'Been slicker 'n snot.' ... huntin' turtles at Johnson's Pond. Only I need to tell you something important —"

"Do not use such phrasing. You need to set a good example for the new baby. Am I right?"

"Yes, sir."

"Tell me about this new friend."

"Dwight's daddy is a big man about town, Dwight Wilcox the Third."

"Wilcox? Dear Lord." Papa wipes his forehead with one of those red gas station rags.

"His daddy calls me, 'Miss Missadelphia.' "

"Is that right?" There's mysterious suspicion in his tone. "So, what's the allure out there at Johnson's Pond?"

He's not really asking about turtles or Johnson's Pond. Two can play this dodgy game. "I forgot to tell you, Dwight's mama is president of the Ladies Auxiliary at Free Will Baptist."

"It's not his mother I'm worried about."

"Papa, we didn't shoot no turtles! Dwight's mama wouldn't allow us no bullets for Dwight's twenty-two. He just likes lugging around an empty rifle."

"There's no such thing as a empty gun, you hear me? Did you do anything useful today?"

"Well … we came by the Super Service, Dwight and me, but you were too busy to even notice. Dwight said, 'Your pap's busier than a one-legged man in a butt-kicking contest.' I tried not to laugh. But I need to tell you something important."

"Summer school's sounding like a real option for you, Little Miss Missadelphia."

"*Ahh* Papa, I don't need no summer schooling."

"Might cure that sudden plague of double negatives."

"Can't we NOT change the subject?"

He laughs. "Go ahead, what's the new subject?"

"Why does it say, 'No Raccoons Allowed' on your restroom door?"

"Raccoons?" He glances at the paint can and slides it behind the desk with his foot.

"Raccoons don't use toilets," I say.

Papa clears his throat, "You make a good point. The mayor himself wanted those signs. That surprise you?" Then he suddenly pretends to get busy.

He opens a desk drawer and takes out a journal-like book. Under the column labeled "Cash Receipts," he writes $150.12.

With a worrisome face, he says, "Those signs are an insult to our colored citizens and a slur against Missadelphia itself … that word." He stands and sits on the corner of the desk. "Sometimes people do dumb things to make themselves feel safer."

"What's the mayor afraid of?"

"Losing his mayor's job is my guess. If and when his colored citizens exercise their right to vote."

"All right, but what's that got to do with his restrooms … and what are Freedom Riders?"

Papa's silent for a moment. "Freedom Riders are fools. Whites and Negroes riding Greyhound buses, whites in the back, Negroes upfront, unmindful of color, fools, brave fools … but I'm afraid people are going to die."

I remember seeing that burning Greyhound bus on the front page of the Clarion-Ledger. "Freedom Riders are like Jim and Huck on their raft; they're brave fools too. Freedom Riders are about irrigation."

"It's pronounced integration, and yes that's what they're claiming."

"Dwight's the one I wouldn't allow access to the mayor's restroom, he peed in your sink ... well, that's what he told me ... I tried not to laugh."

"That's enough about Dwight."

The phone rings. This time I stomp my foot. "I need to tell you something important!"

"Hold on, Leigh ... Mayor's Super Service! ... Oh, Mayor Riggs, what can I do for you?"

No longer willing to be forestalled, I spill it. "Something bad happened at Johnson's Pond. Dwight and me meet up with this colored boy." That gets Papa's attention. "Dwight takes aim with his gun, says, 'We caught us a runaway.'"

The mayor's voice keeps coming through the phone, "Here's what you're gonna do —"

"That colored boy says nothing, just glares mean-like at Dwight and me —"

"Galen, y'all redo the signs, here's the added text —"

"Dwight squeezes the trigger — "

"Hello-hello? Galen, you there?"

"Mayor, hold on, I'm trying to follow two conversations at the same time."

"*Click* goes the gun ... on account of no bullets. I was scared. Dwight laughed. He called that boy ... you know Papa, that word that means 'slave.' "

"Stay away from the Wilcox boy." He picks up the phone, "As for you, Mayor, I will not fix your signs."

"Who is'ts signs your paychecks, boy?"

"I've got to go. There's a busload of Freedom Riders pulling into the Super Service and we're fixin' to serve up sweet tea and cucumber sandwiches, putting the 'service' in Super Service."

"You can't be making jokes at times like these, boy. Wilcox hears, he'll firebomb something, likely my gas station."

"Wilcox sounds like a murderous nitwit."

"The school board will fire your ass, Galen. What the hell are you thinking? You got a baby on the way."

"Your board does not own my ass."

My head's spinning on account of two angry men.

"Calm down," the mayor's saying, "you're taking this the wrong way —"

"You called me 'boy.' What does that mean?"

"It means I was careless."

"Once is careless. Twice sends a message."

"Stop being a jackass."

"Let's try this, Mayor … have the sheriff arrest Wilcox before someone gets hurt."

"He's kin, Wilcox."

Papa slams the telephone down, and after a long moment looks at me with furious eyes. "What are we going to do now, Leigh?"

"I … I know! Let's get on the Freedom Riders bus and ride it all the way to … where's it goin'?"

"New Orleans."

"You, me and Mama … New Orleans folk like band music?"

He hides his face in both hands.

"What's wrong, Papa? Can't we be brave fools?"

Author's Note:

This story is slightly autobiographical. As a teen, while on a family road trip, I did see that horrible sign, crudely painted on a gas station door in eastern Arkansas. Also, my father was a high school band director who, like Galen, worked summers pumping gas and other odd jobs. And Mom claimed kinship to the real General Cleburne. I must credit fellow Brookside writer Gigi Benson for her own fortitude and suggestions, making this a better story.

In Africa Once

By Dan Eeds

October 17, 1950

Dearest Kate,

I hope this missive will finally set matters straight between us. I want you to know that I am devastated by guilt, entirely destroyed. I can say it now; I was wrong from the start. Yes, you pleaded with me not to bring Nigel along with us to Africa. Yes, it was too hot and humid for one so young, as you predicted. The bugs were huge and plentiful, the diseases exotic, the accommodations unspeakable, etc. We both knew how Nigel withered even in London's tepid heat waves.

So I apologize for all the mistakes made.

Poor boy, our angel with the golden curls, lost forever. Each thought the other was watching. Nonetheless, who could have anticipated that the pride of lions would be as curious of Nigel as he was of them? Ha! None of those horrid beasts had ever seen the likes of Nigel before, I am sure of it.

I now sense you never accepted my assurance that the African food chain would not include the likes of our golden boy. And quite right you were. "Safe as a salad," I foolishly said at the time. You know me, always witty while making a sound point. My dearest, it was only said to reassure you. You seemed so damn nervous the whole trip. And now you claim our little safari was a pretext. That hurts me deeply, Kate, for what it implies. I was very fond of Nigel even though he seemed more yours than mine. There was a real attraction between us. Remember that night we came back to my flat and found him snuggly curled inside the remains of my mohair jacket? I was touched, my tears genuine.

Bloody hell, Kate, what do you say? It has been over a month now, will you see me?

All my love,
Terence

P.S. Another fond remembrance: all those calicos and tabbies treed in the park. (How is that for irony?) I can see and hear it all — what a scene! His happy tail wagging as he leaps against the trunk of some ancient elm, the flying slobber, the incessant barking ... our undaunted pooch.
P.P.S. Thursday for tea?

Columbus: Lost in Paradise

Excerpts From a Young Adult Novel
By Dan Eeds

Columbus: Lost in Paradise
Excerpts From a Young Adult Novel

Cast of Characters (in order of appearance):

Fernando Columbus, 14, son of Christopher Columbus and the story's narrator
Pero (ghost boy), 14, orphaned Sevilla street kid
Capitan Mendez, 28, captain of La Capitana
Christopher Columbus (El Admirante) 52, the Admiral

Columbus: Lost in Paradise

Chapter 1, Ghost Boy

By Dan Eeds

Sevilla, Spain, April 10, 1502

Zigzagging my way through morbid gawkers, I see the bodies piled high like marketplace fish, all with gaping mouths and frozen stares. I'm already in a devil of a hurry when the death cart gets itself stuck under the Calle Trabajo archway. I hate Sevilla, the so-called port city to the New World. Hate its narrow streets; hate its teetering three-story apartments; hate its lazy river. Most of all, I hate its hot stench of piss, which today is so foul that horses tremble and grown men weep.

There's no weeping for me, not when my father El Admirante likens tardiness to stealing. "A minute late is the same as picking my pocket," he's fond of saying.

Crouching like a sprinter, I make ready to blow past the stuck cart and its idiot driver. "*Rápido, uno, dos —*" Jostled from behind, I spin and confront an enormous mustache. Hands sweep over my shoulders and down my sleeves. The man's face is so close I can taste the raw onions on his breath as his fingers wrap themselves around my wrists.

Kidnappers!

Twisting free and fired by panic, I swing wildly. The man ducks and laughs, and as he does, I spin and my boot wallops him in the ass. *Ha,* take that!

He doesn't flinch. One of his henchmen says, "It's him — the boy Fernando, see his leather boots and doublet." The ruffians push in for closer inspection, encircling me. I dodge sideways but get tossed back into their midst. With my heart pounding like cannons, the mustached man proclaims, "The Son of El Admirante!" You'd think he'd discovered New World gold. Then with his nose pressed to mine, he dares to add, "Only the bastard son, but he'll do."

I'd been warned not to venture out alone in Sevilla. But testing one's courage requires the risking of life and limb. Stealing apples or swimming naked in the Guadalquivir are mere boys' antics compared to exploring the streets of Sevilla. Better yet, sail the Ocean Sea in one of my father's two-masted, 70-foot caravellas. Small Ship + Large Sea = Proof of Courage.

How can one be the hero of his own story without courage?

A woman screams, a drunkard's jug shatters and the kidnapping thugs freeze like statues.

From the corner of my eye, I see movement inside the death cart. At first, the corpses seem very well behaved, that is to say, silent and still. A man, facedown with rope burns seared into his neck — a thief. A charred slag of ash and bone — *ay,* that one's a witch! And a boy, about my own age, 13 perhaps. With his stick-legs dangling off the cart, with his jutting tongue and eyes locked in death's stare, surely he's suffered a horrible death. But even in death, there's something about those eyes —

"*Que diablos!*" Those eyes flicker to life and turn on me. The boy rises, smiles wickedly, and points a bony finger, curling it in a beckoning gesture that says, "Come join me on the death cart."

This is no kind invitation but the Devil's trick.

This can't be happening. My magnificent imagination is getting the better of me. But then why have the mustached *gamberro* and his men fallen on their knees? Why are they mumbling prayers and clinging to one another in terror?

Light as a spirit, the ghost drops from the cart and comes at me with outstretched arms, "Fer-nan-do, I've been waiting for you."

A shiver runs through me, threatening to explode into full-blown panic. As for courage, I concentrate on not pissing myself.

Chapter 30, The Darkness I Fear

By Dan Eeds

June 25, 1503, off the North Coast of Jamaica.

Thick with Indians, Jamaica. Just this morning, La Capitana's lookout cries, "Smoke, five degrees off port!"

"I know this village," El Admirante says.

Indeed, the smoke is from Village Huareo. Years ago, Cacique Huareo and my father made history together — their Battle of the 70 Canoes. My father's blank cannon salvos scattered the Cacique's canoes, although they were no worse for wear. Rallying, the canoes returned with gifts of fresh fish and bread for my father and his men.

But that was then, and this is now. And now the Cacique has the upper hand — he just doesn't know it yet. He doesn't know about our dire need for safe harbor. Or that my father has his heart set on occupying a beach within a mile of his village. Meanwhile, our sailors mistake my father's foresight for madness. Shrill-tongued, they're saying, "We will die on Jamaica. Let us continue to Santo Domingo." But the colonial capital is hundreds of leagues away against wind and current. And with our cargo hold heavy with seawater, a passing squall could send La Capitana to the bottom with all hands and a great sigh.

True, even on Jamaica our survival is not certain. Upon arrival, per El Admirante's order, our men are not allowed beyond their ship and the adjacent beach camp. There'll be no roving bands of sailors running into Indian houses stealing whatever they want. Spanish sailors have many qualities, but blindly following orders is not one of them. It's been a month since our Belen River disaster in Panama, yet my nights are still haunted by sailors' corpses prickling with arrows. One shouldn't dwell on such dreadful things, but any day now I expect to die.

"Fernando," Pero says, "you're wearing your misery mask." So far this morning we'd loaded the stoves with kindling and did the officers' laundry. "Come, I want to show you something amazing."

I follow my friend to El Admirante's cabin. Head in hands, my father's hunched over his map table. I put a finger to my lips. Never disturb El Admirante when he's working on his maps.

"I think he's asleep," Pero says.

"*Shush.*"

Pero opens the lid of my sea chest. Nestled inside for safekeeping are his own meager things. As he rummages inside an old flour sack, he whispers, "God talked to me last night." His face suddenly gleams, "Found it!" He kisses *it* — a stick wrapped with string and tied off with a fishhook.

"God told you to go fishing?"

"Follow me."

We hurry back to the main deck before the duty officer takes notice of our absence. Between the two of us, we manage to lift the cargo hold hatch. I hold my breath against the wafting stench and peer down into the black water, dreading what I might see. Certainly not cargo, which is stored high-and-dry above deck these days.

Glancing at the fishing line in Pero's hand, I say, "You can't be serious."

He gives me an imbecilic grin as he plays out the fishing line into the hold. "*Ay!*" He yelps and leaps to his feet. "The line's not sinking. We forgot to add a lead weight."

"*We?* It was your dream."

He goes all shifty-eyed. "I'll be right back."

"Wait!"

Alone, I'm guarding the open hatch. Suppose the bosun catches me dawdling? Lashes are a punishment so severe that a less promising boy would flee. Me, I'm clever. Down on hands and knees, I'm scrubbing furiously at an imaginary stain when I hear squeaking noises coming from inside the cargo hold.

Eek, rats! So many they're clinging to each other for dear life. No, the live rats are hanging on to their drowned brother and sister rats, using them for life rafts. God's teeth! It's a rat flotilla. I ponder the meaning of this ongoing tragedy. Is it a vision? An omen? A harbinger of our own doom? Or is it rats just being rats?

Then one rat attempts to shimmy up Pero's fishing line, madly clawing and squeaking, sadly to no gain.

Hurriedly, unthinkingly, I run, grab the nearest storm tether, and drop it into the hold as a rope ladder. Nothing happens. "Stupid rats!" I shout in frustration and begin twirling the tether across the surface of the water like a lasso until one rat grabs on. Excited by my success, I jerk the tether too hard and knock the rat back in the hold.

The rat looks up at me with its beady eyes and says, "Who's stupid now?" At least that's what I imagine it saying. I curse and cast the tether again. Slowly, tether and rat emerge from the hold. The rat leaps for joy and scurries off across the deck to freedom.

Again, back into the hold goes the tether. This time, I land three rats on the deck with one cast. I think this is more fun than real fishing when I hear, "Fernando!"

I nearly jump out of my skin. The Capitan and the bosun are standing over me.

"Unsatisfactory performance, Ensign," Capitan Mendez says.

The bosun is more direct. "What the hell are you doing?"

"*Uhh* —" Fear's got my tongue in a knot. Ensigns outrank bosuns, but it counts for little when the ensign is 14 years old.

"Life is hard when you're stupid, *ay* Fernando?"

"Si, Capitan."

The bosun holds up two fingers. "It takes two sailors to lift that hatch cover."

"*Umm*," Mendez nods in agreement and gives the bosun a dismissing nod. And as the bosun leaves, Pero comes charging back. Snagged by the arm, Pero gets spun about in a half-circle.

"The accomplice," the bosun says. "I say we throw them both into the cargo hold and close the hatch."

Shaking his finger at us, Capitan Mendez says, "I will deal with you later." Again, he gives the bosun permission to leave. Then focusing on Pero and me, he whispers, "Prepare yourselves. We may have to fight our way onto the beach before the day is over."

76

That's unexpected. I'm oddly relieved. Do I fear ship punishment more than Indians? Of course, I fear my father most of all. His words cut deeper than lashes. "Capitan Mendez, it's an officer's duty to be prepared for a battle," I say.

"Indeed."

After helping us replace the hatch, Mendez stretches his back and groans. For an instant, his brow furrows over weary eyes. "After we land, I'll be going on the island."

Dumbfounded, I gasp, "No, the island and the village are forbidden."

"Pardon me? I'm El Admirante's official envoy to the Taino."

"*Sí?* What is … the Taino?"

"What is envoy?" Pero asks.

"Envoy, messenger, I'm on a goodwill mission for our starving crew. I'll barter for fresh provisions while offering the hand of friendship to the people of Jamaica. Every one of whom, from toddling child to teetering codger, fancies himself a warrior … or a farmer, or a fisherman."

Pero whistles in astonishment. "Capitan Mendez, envoy me a side of pork, a few oranges, a wheel of cheese, some marzipan, some —"

"So," Mendez interrupts Pero's shopping list, "tell me about the cargo hold."

I glare at Pero, clueing Capitan Mendez that opening the cargo hold was Pero's idea.

Pero stoops and scoops a cupped hand full of the foul water. "In my dream, God turned La Capitana's rats into fish — beautiful golden dorados longer than my arm."

I'm suddenly dizzy. Blame my dizziness on our starvation diet. I like to dip my infested biscuits in vinegary wine. The weevils are crunchy with a bitter tang of iron. You're tempted to swallow them whole except they tickle on the way down. As for the worms, you'd hardly notice them except for the buttery burst they leave on your tongue. One day I broke my biscuit into pebbled-size bits, scattering them in my palm for close scrutiny. My father said, "Stop playing with your food."

I said, "I'm preparing *Le Biscuit Avec Vers et Charançons.*"

He said, "I suppose they do taste better in French."

Then I told him about my discovery that worms are actually baby weevils. As he pondered this profound idea, I quickly added, "Weevils lay eggs in biscuit flour ... but I am not sure which comes first weevils or weevil eggs." His face turned apoplectic.

In response to Pero's fish dream, I scornfully say, "And what would God have us use for bait, *las cu-ca-rachas?*"

Mendez closes his eyes and silently rubs his temples. "It's my idea that the Taino people are not Indians, but a new people hitherto known only to God." Capitan Mendez clears his throat and smiles sheepishly. "Don't tell El Admirante we've had this little talk. He doesn't want to hear my idea. My point is, out of respect for our new Taino subjects, I choose not to use the word Indian, and neither will you, at least not while you're on their island."

"We are not allowed on their island," I say. "And by the way, Jamaica is my father's island."

Mendez shrugs. "You know how El Admirante's mind is always working on the next scheme? Or should I say, strategic plan? He wants you tagging along, Fernando, whenever I go to the village." Mendez quickly adds, "But not the first visit, it could be —"

"Dangerous?"

Pero interrupts. "It will be good to get off the ship, no?"

"*Silencio*, Capitan Mendez is talking to me, not to you."

"Did you know that Taino means The Good People?" Mendez puts an arm around each of our shoulders and looks us in the eyes. "So ... " His voice trails off, his face softens into a smile.

"Ty-EE-no," Pero says, practicing this new word.

"The Good People," I say.

It's good that Capitan Mendez is so young. He remembers how difficult it is being a boy.

Chapter 31, Trouble at the Tiller

By Dan Eeds

All during midday, La Capitana limps towards her final destination, our new Jamaican home. But first, there's a treacherous inlet to navigate. Pero and I are at the helm with El Admirante and Capitan Mendez, meeting with the pilot and his tillerman, planning this tricky passage. The best approach is straight-on rather than angling our way. Once inside the narrow inlet, there'll be no room for maneuvering. La Capitana must aim for the true flight of an arrow.

As the meeting ends, Capitan Mendez asks if I have anything to add.

How easy it is to make a fool of one's self. I answer, "*Sí,* let's find another beach without a dangerous inlet."

Mendez compounds my error, asking, "Why this beach?"

Father's eyes are fixed on Mendez, but I feel his real focus is on me because it's my chin that's being pinched between his thumb and finger. "That is a poor question, Capitan Mendez. Tell him, Fernando, tell Capitan the good answer."

I give Mendez a forlorn glance. "Inside the reef is a bay offering protection from storms, a stream for freshwater, an estuary with abundant game, and most importantly, there is the Indian village." I want to be somewhere, anywhere else. So, I stare at the tillerman, a giant of a man, Andrius from Antwerp, who's sniffling, seemingly on the verge of tears. "What's wrong with you?" I ask bluntly, hoping to divert my father's attention.

Andrius stares at his hands and with a trembling chin, says, "La Capitana handles like a dead whale, a worm-eaten hulk. Today is her last day at sea, forever."

"*Sí*, it's a sorrowful day," Pero and I agree.

Andrius nods. "*Ja-ja.*"

Well, the pilot cares not for Andrius' sad lament. Perhaps he's embarrassed by it. "You wretch, in this calm sea, anyone could handle the tiller."

Andrius is silent for a moment, then, out of the blue, asks if Pero and I would like to "work the tiller" on this calm sea day.

The pilot hotly objects. "Remember the Santa Maria? Christmas Eve, 1492? A boy at the tiller?"

Capitan Mendez jumps in. "Allowing the drunken crew to celebrate the birth of the Savior. But today, we have El Admirante's son and his able assistant."

My father is silent as the Santa Maria was one of his ships, her entire crew lost.

I suspect there's some petty feud between the pilot and his tillerman. (Later, Father explains that pilots are famously snobbish as they are the only sailors tested and certified by the Crown of Spain.)

So, Andrius stations Pero at the starboard bulwark and me at the port, 6 feet apart, with the tiller between us. The tiller is an 8-foot wooden handle bolted to the rudder through a shaft in the helm port. Each of us has our own block and tackle assembly. A tiller without block and tackle would be unruly even for a giant like Andrius from Antwerp. B&Ts operate mechanically, employing pulley and rope to dampen the power of the sea while boosting the power of the tillerman.

"Fernando, it's not a tug of war," Capitan Mendez shouts.

"Pero's fighting me for control of the tiller … he's not a good tillerman."

"Maybe it's the other way around!" Pero whines.

But La Capitana is beginning to change course, her bow turning towards the island. I shudder with a thrilling sense of power.

"Don't look at the island … listen to Andrius," Capitan Mendez warns.

Andrius directs Pero and me in his heavily accented Spanish: "Pero, starboard your helm, easy now. Fernando, more, much more, forward, that's it, better, ease up Fernando, again, more slack Pero! Fernando, steady, steady, now port."

Presently, there's a deep rumbling. On port and starboard sides, waves break across a seemingly endless reef with exposed coral heads. At eye level, toppling waves surge and meld with jagged coral, hissing as if poured over molten lava and sending plumes of spray into the helm through cutouts in the bulwark.

"Fernando!" Someone shouts. The pilot, up till now silent, curses with some very naughty words.

"Fernando, pull!" The tiller swings hard into my chest, knocking me on my ass. The long legs of Andrius step over me, brushing aside my outstretched hand. He takes my place at the tiller with the mountains of Jamaica looming closer, darker and more threatening.

"Threading the eye of a needle with a dead whale," Andrius says with newfound joy.

"*Ja-ja,*" Capitan Mendez agrees.

Suddenly we're inside a quiet, flat-water bay, our home for the foreseeable future. But the pilot glowers at Capitan Mendez. "There'll be consequences for your abuse of my authority."

"While you're at it, write a letter to the Queen," Mendez says. "Good work, lads — we learn by doing." He gives the unhappy pilot a slap on the back. "You too, I'll make a good report to the boy's father."

"So, where's my Uncle Barto's ship?" I ask.

"*Ahh,* the Santiago, I forgot all about her." Mendez turns, his eyes search beyond the reef to the horizon where clouds are stacking themselves into minarets. His face is disturbingly calm as if shipwrecking is a Capitan's routine duty. "She'll be along soon," he sighs.

We leave the helm, but the drama is just beginning. La Capitana plows on towards the beach, almost vibrant in the following wind. Despite a flooded cargo hold, she's picking up speed with all sails unfurled. When Capitan Mendez hurries by, Pero and I give chase. Glancing over my shoulder, I see Andrius alone at the helm with his arms outstretched like a giant crucifix. At that instant I realize that at the tiller, I had acted as his right arm and Pero his left.

Relieved of helmsman duty, I'm free to study the serenity of the bay. I have a sensation of flying as we pass over patchworks of rippled sand, cobalt-blue holes, and coral mounds in shades of orange and yellow where scores of radiantly blue fish dart helter-skelter, startled by our passing.

When El Admirante next makes his appearance on deck, he's hobbling. "Ay, napping is not kind to old men," the admiral complains as he stretches his back muscles. Nonetheless, he's urging the crew. "Look alive … keep a good watch!" With the beach now less than a hundred yards away, our crewmen stand ready with buckled swords as they line both rails.

"Landing party, ready!" Capitan Mendez shouts.

"Prepare for collision!" commands El Admirante.

I'm ready too: tethered up for our beach collision. But my eyes stray to the forested mountains, scanning up and down the shore and along the tree line. Searching for what? Hidden painted faces? The glint of a spearhead?

Movement! Starboard! A shadow bounds over the wind-driven sand atop the beach, weaving in and out of the trees, stopping, then sprinting forward into sunlight. A girl, possibly human. Waist-up naked, with tattoos, onyx eyes, and a face to launch 70 canoes. She's looking straight at me, or maybe straight through me. I stupidly wave.

If our men see her, they'll become dogs gnawing on the same bone.

For now, at least, all eyes are fixed on the rapidly approaching beach. There's a tremor. La Capitana shudders and groans. Pero's thrown to the deck; Mendez goes down, along with El Admirante. One of the ship's boys flies over the rail and kerplunks into the bay. I purposely lower myself to the deck amongst our fallen crewmen, expecting to hear the horror of swooshing arrows. I cover my neck with both hands, shielding it.

Just as quickly, Capitan Mendez is back on his feet, helping my father. The foolish ship's boy is laughing and treading circles off starboard.

An hour later, Capitan Mendez tosses his head, settling his thick black hair. "La Capitana is moored," he informs El Admirante.

Moored? Her bow is stuck in the sand, still 50 feet short of the beach.

At that moment, there's a shout, and all heads turn to port. The hulk of the Santiago slips almost silently alongside La Capitana, board-by-board close. It's an impressive feat of sailing if running a caravella aground counts as sailing these days.

As for the girl, she's gone. Was she even real? Or was she conjured up by my troubled spirit, an artifact of my desperate hunger?

Chapter 32, Required Reading

By Dan Eeds

The same day, near sunset.

"All hands! El Admirante!" Capitan Mendez announces.

I watch as they crowd around — the crew assembling, on crates, on kegs, sailors riding atop other sailors' shoulders. A disheveled assembly, hollow-faced, clothes hanging off bones like drapes. We are the ghost sailors doomed to never reach our destination.

"Where is Fernando?"

"Here I am, Admirante, sir." I push my way forward through men too exhausted to make way for El Admirante's son.

"Having distinguished himself at the helm today, my son has earned the honor of reading aloud *The Requirement*." He offers me the scroll.

Reluctantly I take it. "These grave words require more authority than mine."

"It's officious nonsense," Capitan Mendez says. "Any fool can exercise that sort of authority."

"What do you have to say for yourself?" El Admirante demands, jabbing his finger in my chest.

"It will cause problems with our new friends, the Taino people."

The crew erupts with laughter at the word "friends."

El Admirante turns to Capitan Mendez. "Where was my son's reticence when he countermanded my order to sail east?"

"You were at death's door that day."

"God's teeth! My son is responsible for my fleet sailing off in the wrong direction."

Mendez glances at me. "Your son exercised sound judgment given the circumstances. We were on the knife's edge of mutiny. The Porras brothers would have you both set adrift at sea. In your stead, Fernando told the mutineers what they wanted to hear, thus preventing a mutiny."

"And here we are, 200 leagues from Santo Domingo. Read *The Requirement*."

"But the Indians will not hear it, and if they hear it, they will not understand," I protest.

My father looks at me with the posture of all great men: chin high, shoulders back. "Read it with detachment. Capitan Mendez is correct. It's a formality."

"But I see no Indians."

"*The Requirement* is not for my Indians. It is for my crew. It forgives our ... lapses ... in advance."

Pero whispers in my ear, "I think he means loud and disorderly conduct, looting, etcetera."

I wave Pero off. "Crimes committed against your Indians? The Savior says, 'Whatsoever you do to the least of my brothers, you do unto me.' He will not be pleased if we mistreat the locals," I warn.

The crewmen give a collective gasp, as if I had just summoned forth Jesus himself to shame them.

Capitan Mendez clears his throat. "It must be read by an officer, and you accepted your ensign commission."

Defeated, I resign myself to an officer's call of duty. I hand the scroll back to my startled father. "It's burned in memory."

"He's memorized it!" my father gloats.

"On behalf of —"

"Louder, Fernando. And face my island."

"But Papa, you said it was for the crew."

I recite from memory what I had heard many times. I shout it to a clump of swaying palm trees. "ON BEHALF OF El ADMIRANTE OF THE OCEAN SEA AND ALL THE LANDS THEREIN —"

I pause, already out of breath.

"WE NOTIFY AND MAKE KNOWN TO YOU THAT THE LORD OUR GOD IS CREATOR OF HEAVEN AND EARTH, CREATOR OF ONE MAN AND ONE WOMAN, OF WHOM YOU AND WE AND ALL THE MEN OF THE WORLD ARE DESCENDANTS."

"That's my favorite part," Pero says.

"No commentary," El Admirante says with severity.

"ALL THOSE NOTIFIED SHALL RECEIVE AND SERVE THEIR MAJESTIES WITH GOODWILL AND WITHOUT ANY RESISTANCE; ALL, OF THEIR OWN FREE WILL, BECOME CHRISTIANS. BUT, IF YOU DO NOT DO THIS, WE CERTIFY THAT WE SHALL MAKE WAR AGAINST YOU, WE SHALL TAKE YOU AND

YOUR WIVES AND YOUR CHILDREN AND SHALL SELL AND DISPOSE OF THEM, AND WE SHALL TAKE AWAY YOUR GOODS AND SHALL DO YOU MISCHIEF AND DAMAGE. THEREFORE, BE IT RESOLVED, THE DEATHS AND LOSSES WHICH SHALL ACCRUE ARE YOUR FAULT AND NOT THAT OF THEIR MAJESTIES OR GODLY SPANIARDS WHO COME WITH US. WE HAVE SAID THIS TO YOU AND MAKE THIS REQUIREMENT."

"*Esta bien,*" my father says. "The notary shall record that all have given witness."

So concludes this dreadful "formality."

    ... *to be continued.*

Michael C. Healy

The Man in the Basement

By Michael C. Healy

There was a strange man living in the basement. Actually, a subterranean world below the basement. Unbeknownst to us, my wife Peggy and me, he'd been living there for years. Our house is located in San Francisco on California Street. It's a fine old three-story Queen Anne Victorian, painted a light buttery yellow with green trim. There are two turrets, one in front with curved bay windows and one in the rear with one window at the top. From there you can get a peek at the bay. Extending a story below ground, the bottom of the back turret serves as a basement.

Inside the house it is old-fashioned opulence with 14-foot ceilings and green velvet drapes defining the windows. I inherited the house two years ago from my Great Aunt Phoebe who passed away at 101 years. It was built in the mid-1800s by Phoebe's great-grandfather, Marshall H. Huntington, an explorer of note at the time. The construction was by shipwrights on shore leave. Not uncommon in those days. As for the workmanship, there is none better. Interestingly, if you stand across the street and close one eye to look straight at the house, there is an optical illusion. It looks like it lists slightly to starboard, reminiscent of an old square-rigger being pushed by a westerly wind. The old gas jets are still there, remnants of a bygone era.

My name is Evan Barksdale. I'm an account executive and junior partner at a small advertising firm on Battery Street.

Great Aunt Phoebe was a strange bird, given to magical thinking. She had once been a beauty.

I remember visiting as a boy and her telling me, *sotto voce*, as if she were afraid we'd be overheard, that the house was the "universe." And one day it would be mine and I would know its secrets. She also said the house dwelled in a time warp. Even to a 12-year-old, which I was at the time, it sounded like gobbledygook. I chalked it up to her being a crazy old lady.

Father was kinder and used the word "eccentric." I remember on one of my visits she showed me her treasured photo album of my ancestors. It was filled with sepia-toned photos of members of the Huntington family. There was Marshall Huntington, the family patriarch, in a dark waistcoat and top hat, and son Horatio, in similar dress. Then one of Horatio and his wife Gertrude. They both looked sour.

"Horatio disappeared," Phoebe had said. She giggled. "It was a scandal. Something about his wife's death."

I had only seen Aunt Phoebe once since I was about 14 or 15 and that was with Peggy. So, it was a surprise when I learned from her lawyer I had actually inherited the house.

One morning I discovered by accident a secret room under the bottom of the rear turret. The only access to that section of the turret was from the utility room in the back of the house, off the kitchen. Wooden stairs led down into the turret basement. I had built a little wine rack down there on one side because it was the coolest place in the house. On Friday evening before my discovery we had friends over for dinner and I went down to get a vintage bottle of Cabernet Sauvignon. While down there I heard noises coming from under the turret's planked floor. The sound was muffled because there is a thin oriental throw rug covering most of the floor. I figured it was rats and would deal with the little bastards the next day, Saturday. I got up early and headed back down to hunt for those noisy rodents, a couple of traps in hand.

The bottom of that back turret was pitch black. I hit the switch for the one naked lightbulb hanging from a rafter, which cast eerie shadows along the walls. Again, I heard a noise coming from beneath my feet. I rolled up the rug, but needed more illumination to see what I was doing. I got a high-powered flashlight to search the floor for a loose plank. Instead I found a trap door with a sliver of light coming through the cracks around the sides. My heart began to race and I just sat there numb for a moment. This was incredible. Something or someone was down there moving about. How was this even possible? I went and got an old Smith & Wesson .38 that had belonged to my father, who had passed away five years before. It was just for show. It did not have a firing pin.

After a few tense moments, I found a well-hidden steel handle folded down in a slot and pulled the planked door up toward me to reveal the hidden room below. There were stairs and I went down a few steps so that I could see better. And what I saw was a large subterranean dwelling, fully lighted. There were pictures hanging on the walls, a sagging brown couch, a desk and chairs. A middle-aged man with a full salt-and-pepper beard was standing at a small kitchen counter. He was pouring something into a cup.

"Hello, Evan," the man said without looking at me, as if I was an old friend, come to call. "I've been expecting you now for about two years. Ever since you moved in. You've been a little slow."

"Who are you and what are you doing here?"

"Come on down," the man said. "I've just brewed some tea. Do you like tea?"

I just stared at him — my blood felt like it was coursing through me at Mach 6 speed.

"How long have you been here?" I said, the shock of finding him affecting the timbre of my voice. It felt like I was swallowing my words, which made them sound hollow to me.

"Let's see, since Sunday, June 18, 1882, at seven o'clock in the evening."

I laughed.

"That's absurd," I said. "You really expect me to believe that? That would make you ..."

"Actually, if you go strictly by the clock I'm 181 years old. I was born in 1839 in a tent. Father built this house in 1854. When Phoebe passed away I was glad to learn someone in the family was moving in. As you can see, I'm quite cozy down here, while waiting to make contact."

I gingerly came down the rest of the way to the bottom.

"I have a gun," I said.

"Really," he said.

I showed him the gun which I had pulled out of my belt. He looked at it and shrugged.

"Okay, you have a gun," he said. "You can put it away now. There's no threat here."

He shook his head as if he were dealing with a child.

"How about that tea," he said.

"What's your name?"

"I'm sorry, I forgot to introduce myself," he said. "I'm Horatio B. Huntington."

I just shook my head, but then remembered the old photo album.

"What was your father's name?"

"Marshall Huntington," simply rolled off his tongue.

"Phoebe's great-grandfather? Didn't he discover a tribe of Pygmies in the Belgian Congo?"

"Very good, Evan." he said. "By the way, you can call me Hunt. It's easier. I've never liked Horatio."

I looked carefully at this man who called himself Horatio B. Huntington and was amazed to see that in fact the resemblance to the picture in Aunt Phoebe's album, which I had looked at again recently, was uncanny. Even with the beard. He was clean shaven in the picture.

"So, what relation was Phoebe to you?"

"My granddaughter, of course."

"She told me you had disappeared because of something having to do with your wife."

"That's next on the agenda," he said blithely.

Now I was intrigued. This guy was either a total lunatic or a very crafty con artist who did some research on the family and found himself a cheap place to live, and created this ridiculous fiction about himself. But he struck me as harmless. I stuffed the gun back in my pants.

Playing along, I asked him how he could possibly have lived so long?

"Ah," he said," handing me a cup of tea. "I don't know the answer to that. It's a quirk in the cosmos. But I have a theory. Think of this place as a kind of wormhole where time and space are all jumbled up. And within it is a time warp and for some very strange reason time for me was suspended. You see, I'm really only 43 years old. It's like I'm in a holding pattern. My wife Gertrude, Phoebe's grandmother, was murdered in 1882 and found in an upstairs bedroom of this house. Apparently poisoned. I knew the police would suspect me. We were not getting along, plus I dabbled in chemistry. So, I came down here to hide as soon as I learned what had happened and have been here ever since. This was once a room I used as my lab.

"Did you do it?" I said and almost kicked myself for acting like he was for real.

"I couldn't prove I didn't," he said. "Very difficult to prove a negative. Try your tea."

I took a sip and discovered it was very good.

"Well," I said, as if I believed him, "did you, or didn't you?"

"Of course, I didn't," he said. "It was never solved. I always believed it was her lover, Jason Margolo. As a matter of fact, you look like him. Anyway, the authorities learned I knew about the affair and believed I had killed her in a jealous rage. However, you don't poison someone in a jealous rage. It's a method that has to be planned. Frankly, I couldn't have cared less. The marriage was as empty as a whore's dream. Believe me, Gertrude was not meant to live with a man born of a woman. What I needed then and still need is a solid alibi."

As I listened to this rubbish I realized for a moment I was getting sucked into this guy's delusions.

"How do you get supplies, food and stuff?" I said.

"I steal it from you in the dead of night or when you are out, but not enough so's you'd notice. There is another portal, so to speak, an entry and exit from here."

"What?" I said.

He pointed to a heavy timbered door at the far end of the room and told me that it led to an underground corridor that circled back in time to this very house in 1882 and the night they found Gertrude's body. He said she was discovered by one of the house staff. At that time, the house belonged to his family, he said. Hunt said Gertrude and he lived on the third floor and his mother and father on the second floor. Being a famous explorer, his father was rarely there.

"I have to stay within the wormhole," he said. "Otherwise I would instantly disintegrate."

"Right," I said. "Of course."

Hunt smiled.

"You're patronizing me," he said. "I understand your skepticism, I suppose I would question such a story if our situations were reversed."

"Well," I said. "Keep the noise down. I'm not going to tell my wife you're down here. I'm afraid she'll have a tantrum."

"I understand," he said. "I've heard some of her shrill tirades, even from down here. Her voice reminds me of Gertrude."

I turned to go.

"Evan," he said. "Before you leave, would you like to go with me?"

"Go where with you?"

"Through the tunnel, back through time to this house in 1882."

I put my cup of tea back down on the table and stared at this psychopath.

"It only takes a short while, an hour at most," he said. "I mean you can't beat going back almost 140 years in an hour."

"You're going to take me back to this house in 1882, is that what I'm hearing?"

Hunt nodded.

"Think of it as an amazing discovery," he said. "An insanely exciting peregrination."

"A what?"

"A journey, like no other," Hunt said.

I put my foot on the first step of the stairs. I was ready to climb back up to the basement of the turret as fast as possible, where some semblance of reality prevailed.

"Please come back for tea some time," Hunt said. "I do get lonely for company."

I just shook my head and wondered if I was just dreaming this, half expecting to wake up at any time. But it was all too vivid. As I reached the top of the stairs Hunt called up to me that he enjoyed finally meeting me.

"Did Phoebe know you were here?" I said.

"Of course," he called up to me. "She was an alchemist, you know. She knew everything."

"An alchemist," I repeated. "Right."

"Let me know if you change your mind," he yelled. I replaced the trap door and then the rug.

Peggy was in the kitchen making some coffee. She looked thin and pale. She was wearing a housecoat and slippers. Her mousy hair, which had some advancing gray in it, was tousled. It looked like a fright wig sitting on top of her head.

"What are you doing, Evan?" she demanded.

"Nothing, dear. Just puttering around."

"Really," she said with a tone that always made me feel I was under attack. "You look like the cat that swallowed the canary. I thought I heard voices."

"Couldn't have, dear," I said. "I was just checking something in the utility room."

"What?"

"Nothing, I … I wanted to get a clean towel out of the hamper."

"Where is it?"

"Where is what?"

"The towel, dummy," she said. "What's the matter with you?!"

"Oh, I must have left it down there," I said.

Peggy rolled her eyes heavenward and poured her coffee.

"You're really impossible," she said. "Stay out of the laundry. Cloe will be here to do it later."

Cloe Sanchez was our cleaning lady. She came three times a week, splitting up the work between downstairs and the upper floors. She'd been with us for some time.

I went out to the drawing room which was just off the vestibule. I sat and stared into space, wondering how much longer I was going to be able to endure Peggy. The marriage, if you could call it that, had liquefied at least 10 years back, maybe more. Peggy had not wanted children. She had made that clear right from our first date, which in hindsight was also a little presumptuous. I mean she came right out with that statement as if we were engaged. The truth was I pretended that was okay with me, but in reality, I did want children. When we did get engaged after a few months of courtship, if

101

you want to call it that, I hoped she would change her mind about children. Peggy didn't change her mind. She did not like children, nor dogs or cats either, and most of all sex. So, for years we lived in a lonely vacuum, absent of intimacy of any kind. Not long ago I began hearing a voice in my head that Peggy was plotting against me.

Peggy had a nice face in those early days, but over the years it had gotten twisted from her latent and not so latent anger. There was something even vulgar about her face. The look of her mouth, once full and sensuous, had shriveled into a constant thin-lipped sneer. I never really knew what the source of her anger was, nor her resentment of me. It seemed so deeply ingrained in every fiber of her being and didn't really show itself until our second year of marriage. Possibly it stemmed from something in her childhood. An abusive father or mother. Who knew? I was not a psychologist. I'd asked her more than once why she was constantly in a state of anger.

"I'm not in a state of anger," she would reply, always with a sharp edge. "I see things for what they are. I see our life together for what it is."

One thing it was, was her pushing us toward bankruptcy. She was spending what precious money we had at a rapid rate. Mostly on things for herself, new clothes to impress her friends, all top-of-the-line stuff. She had to be stopped, I thought. A day of reckoning. The voice again.

I pressed on.

"Oh!" I said. "What is it, dear? Our life for what it is?"

She looked at me with what I interpreted as disgust.

"A dark abyss," she said, absently. "You stole my best years, Evan."

We were sitting at the breakfast nook having coffee at that moment. I took a sip from my cup, then slowly put it down.

"Really," I said. "Do you remember we had sex in my car on our third date, at your insistence, then you demanded that we get married. And after that sex was in short supply."

"Don't be coarse, Evan."

Peggy stood up and walked to the door.

"I don't need to listen to this garbage," she said and went upstairs to her bedroom.

It occurred to me that maybe she didn't even recognize the rage in herself, not to mention a faulty memory. When I brought Peggy once to meet Aunt Phoebe, not long before Phoebe's death, it was like butter wouldn't melt in her mouth, as they say. But later when we had left she turned to me in the car and said: "What's with that old looney great aunt of yours?" She said it jokingly, but I felt at the time she meant it in an unkind way. I simply said she could seem odd.

For a few years Phoebe did have a live-in companion she had met in Tibet. His name was Aimilios. According to Phoebe he was actually from the Hunza Valley, high in the Himalayas, and a descendent of Alexander the Great. I remember seeing him at the house on some of my visits when father would drop me off. Aimilios was tall and exotic looking with a swarthy complexion and penetrating black eyes. I remember those eyes. I always felt that he could look right through me when he was around. He always wore a white cap with a feather in it, and a tunic over the shiny pajama-like pants. Aimilios was even more mysterious than Phoebe. Never spoke in my presence. I wondered where he was or if he was even still alive. He was much younger than Phoebe, not much

103

more than a boy when he first hooked up with her. So, it was possible. Perhaps he went to Tibet, or back to the Hunza Valley.

Later I had some breakfast and then went into the office for a meeting about one of our major accounts. We met in the conference room. The meeting included the creative staff and my partner BJ Ascot. But frankly it was hard to stay focused as I thought about Hunt, living in the lower depths of our house. I was still having trouble believing that I hadn't dreamed the whole thing. And that nonsense about traveling back to the Huntington house in … what was it, 1882. And yet there was something almost matter of fact about his invitation. I could only imagine how Peggy would react if I told her about Hunt. She'd have me carted off. The art director was saying something but the words were like white noise.

"Evan, what do you think?" I heard BJ's voice, which sounded like it was coming from a deep well.

"What?"

"Evan, are you listening?" BJ said. "Where are you?"

I nodded.

"You seem a million miles away."

"Oh, sorry," I said.

Later, after the discussion and staff had left, BJ asked me to step into his office for a chat. When someone says they want to chat about something, I immediately get suspicious that something is wrong. I grabbed some more coffee and went down the hall to BJ's office. It was one of those corner jobs with two giant windows coming together, forming the corner at the joints. He had a panoramic view of the bay, spanning from the Golden Gate Bridge to Treasure Island. It was clearly the best office on the floor, but then he was the senior partner.

When I entered he told me to shut the door behind me. I did, then sat down opposite his desk and took a sip of my coffee. BJ wrote something on a piece of paper then looked up at me, a dour expression etched into his face.

"Evan," he started in this fatherly tone he sometimes took. "Are you happy?"

My coffee nearly went down the wrong way and I coughed a few times.

"Am I what?"

"Happy," he said. "You know, when you generally have a feeling of well-being. Happy."

I didn't answer. It seemed to me to be an absurd question. Also, I could feel a threat welling up deep inside me. What was this guy I'd known for years getting at?

"Are things okay at home between you and Peggy?"

I stood up.

"What the hell business is that of yours?" I blurted.

"Something's affecting your work," BJ said. "I'm concerned."

"Bullshit!" I yelled and wondered if I could be heard outside in the cubicle area.

"You're stressed, Evan," BJ said. "Take some time off."

I threw the half empty paper cup at his desk, what was left of the coffee splashing along the glass top. BJ reared back, almost tipping over backward, a shocked expression on his face.

"What the hell!" he said.

"Fuck you, BJ!" I screamed and walked out, feeling like some hobgoblin was driving me.

I went down the hall to my puny office and stood for a few moments looking around. Then, all of a sudden, in some insane primal action, I reached down with my right hand and swept all the papers, inbox, and telephone off my desk onto the floor. Next, I turned over my desk, more papers from open drawers flying everywhere. I got my briefcase and my coat, and headed for the elevator. I yelled out that I knew there was a conspiracy against me in the office. So-called colleagues were against me. I heard someone say, "Jesus! Evan's gone crazy!" All eyes from the bullpen were on me as I walked briskly toward the front. The last face I saw was BJ's. He'd heard the commotion and stepped out of his office to see what was going on. He stood there and simply watched after me with a sad knowing look on his face. It made me wonder if he and Peggy were plotting something to destroy me. I knew they had secretly met a few times. I knew because I followed her. But I didn't let on that I knew they were meeting. It even occurred to me they might be having an affair.

Back home I went immediately to the kitchen and poured myself a drink, Scotch, straight. Peggy snuck up behind me.

"What are you doing home?" she demanded. "Why aren't you at work? And isn't it a little early to be drinking?"

I whispered: "Shut up!" Really more to myself than to Peggy.

"What did you say?" Peggy said.

"Nothing, dear," I said.

"Well, please keep quiet," she said. "I have friends over for our weekly bridge game. We're in the den."

106

I shut my eyes and pictured that look on BJ's face as I exited the office.

"Is everything okay?" Peggy said.

"Couldn't be better," I said.

She turned and went back to the den. I heard voices giggling. Peggy was probably telling her friends some amusing story about me to entertain them, about how, in fact, she loathed me. Yes, a strong word, but it's true. I could always feel it whenever she walked into a room I was in.

I have to get rid of her, I said aloud. I knew she was dangerous. I would have to strike first.

"*Señor Barksdale, todo bien?*"

I looked up to see Cloe standing there in front of me with a dust mop in her hand.

"Err ... you okay?" she repeated in her broken English.

"What?"

"*Palido!*" she said. "Very pale."

I nodded, walked away and went upstairs to lie down. The phone rang.

Later, Peggy told me BJ called and said I was acting strange. I didn't respond. She then told me she was going to visit her mother and would be home late. I was certain she was really going to meet BJ in some cheap motel for a little tryst. For dinner I heated a can of chili con carne and washed it down with Scotch. I kept thinking about Hunt, about going back to another time. Was it possible? He seemed so sure, so confident, even cavalier about it, as if the idea should not be so foreign to my sense of logic, my perception of the physical world. Sitting in the kitchen I could feel the pull of this strange man in the tiny subterranean world he was living in. I decided to go visit Hunt and test his story.

107

I made my way back down to that dark place at the bottom of the back turret, pulled the throw-rug back and opened the trap door. There was Hunt's little world. I walked slowly down the steps. Hunt was sitting in a club chair smoking. He looked up as I reached the bottom.

"I've been waiting for you, Evan," he said. "Are you ready to take the journey?"

I looked at Hunt, who'd trimmed his beard. He looked much younger now, I thought.

"You're still skeptical," he said as he stood and put out his cigarette.

"Let's just say I'm intrigued."

He told me to follow him and stay close. The tunnel back is very old, he said, and very close.

"Are you claustrophobic?" he asked.

"No."

"Good," he said.

Hunt went to the far end of the room and with some heft, lifted a thick iron crossbar that secured it. He pulled the heavy planked door open. It looked like something from an eighth century castle and squeaked like a banshee out of hell.

"Could use some oil on those hinges," Hunt remarked.

He then stepped into the dark hollow beyond. I hesitated at first, but then followed Hunt through the opening. I felt a little like Alice falling down the rabbit hole. What struck me were the working gas lights every 20 feet or so all along the way. The tunnel floor was uneven cobblestone and the walls and ceiling were reinforced by brick and mortar. It smelled musty, and was dank with the earth's sweat. As we made our way a heavy dampness appeared along the cobblestones.

"Be careful," Hunt said. "It can be a little slippery."

"Who built this tunnel?" I said, my voice echoing into oblivion.

"My father had it built in case there was a need to escape the house. Originally there were two branches. One was built to go down to the old Barbary Coast for drink and entertainment unmolested. There was always the danger of being Shanghaied right off the street and sold to unscrupulous ship captains. That branch is closed off. The other branch, the one we are taking, circles back through time to the house."

"Right, a time warp." I scoffed. "Like science fiction."

"No, like the black hole in space."

"Naturally," I said, not hiding my mounting skepticism.

I mean I found the whole thing incredible, but I was still curious to see where we would actually end up. We moved along at a rapid pace. The tunnel did seem to make jogs here and there. What was particularly eerie was the profound silence except for the sound of our footsteps. It was just under an hour before we reached what looked like that same heavy planked door we had entered. Hunt pushed it open and told me to go through, but that he would be staying just inside the tunnel.

"What?" I said.

"I can't go back until my name is cleared," he said. "And that's what I want you to do, clear my name so I can resume my life in the era I was destined to be in."

"What can I do?" I said.

"Tell them that you are a long-lost friend who ran into me, and that you were with me at the Bella Union drinking and catching up when the murder of my wife, Gertrude, occurred."

I thought, okay, I'll play along with this charade.

"The Bella Union," I repeated. "Okay, where's that?"

Hunt looked at me with a shocked expression,

"Why, it's one of the most famous saloons and gambling places on the Barbary Coast," he said. "If you do this, provide my alibi, I'll do something for you."

"Like what?" I said.

"I have an idea what you would most desire and yet probably have not dared say it to yourself."

I just looked at him, wondering what he was talking about, but in some dark corner of my being, knew perfectly well what he meant.

"Need I spell it out, Evan?" He said. "Peggy, that shrew of a wife of yours," he said.

I said nothing to dissuade him.

It was definitely the same heavy timber door we had entered back in 2021. I just stood there looking at Hunt. He motioned for me to go through the opening. I shook my head thinking this game had gone far enough.

"Well," he said. "What are you afraid of? You should at the very least be curious about what's on the other side."

"Okay," I said. "I'll play along."

With that I stepped through. The room we had left behind now looked very different. It was, and smelled like chemicals. There was a very dim piece of light coming from the other end of the room. I walked slowly toward the light, bumping into a table along the way. It was a very low gas jet sconce. I turned it up to see that the room I was in was a laboratory. There were test tubes, flasks and a microscope on one table. A Bunsen burner, bottles, books on another. It looked a little like the lab in the movie "Frankenstein" I had seen as a kid. I remember the story from Phoebe that

Horatio's father had picked up a Bunsen burner while visiting the University of Heidelberg around 1860, and helped to introduce them to scientists in America.

I immediately thought that I was dreaming, as I looked around. Then I saw the steps, the same steps I had come down from the bottom of the back turret. I went up and pushed open the trap door. As I entered the turret I could hear the muffled sound of men's and women's voices coming from above. It sounded like a lot of people. What were people doing in my house — friends of Peggy's? She didn't have that many friends. Just her bridge club. I went from the turret up the passageway stairs to the utility room. When I came out it was clear that something was very different about the place than when I left it. The kitchen was totally different. Copper pots and pans hung from a rack attached to the ceiling in the middle of the room, and a large old gas burning stove with a porcelain oven door was up against the wall. This was not the kitchen I knew. My nerves were now beginning to tingle.

The voices seemed to be coming from the parlor. I followed them and found a crowd of people standing around chatting. Uniformed police were standing by the door while plain clothes police seemed to be taking statements. I could see that it was dark outside. My watch had stopped. One of the officers by the door saw me and with his extended hand directed me to join the others. I did. A middle-aged woman in a floor-length dark dress noticed me and came over.

"Who are you?" She said. "I don't remember seeing you before."

"I'm an old friend of Hunt's," I said. "We were supposed to meet back here."

"Horatio? Really," the woman said. "I'm his mother. What's your name?"

"Evan," I said.

"Strange, I don't recall him ever mentioning you before," she said. "You say you were supposed to meet him here. The police want to speak to him. A terrible thing has happened. His wife Gertrude has been found dead in the upstairs bedroom. They believe she was murdered." She leaned in close to me. "I'm afraid my son is the chief suspect," she said to me, just above a whisper. "If he did it, I don't blame him, she was an evil witch! The marriage was a merger of families. The police believe she was poisoned with some exotic extract from a South American plant. The medical person said he could smell it and recognized it."

It occurred to me that forensic science was emerging as a significant tool in police investigations even then.

"When do they think this happened?"

"She was alive and running around an hour and a half ago, then said she wasn't feeling well and went upstairs to lie down. The medical person … examiner … believes she took a poisoned drink that acted very fast."

A man in a dark suit approached us, introduced himself as the chief of detectives, Darrel Strong, and addressed Missus Huntington.

"You're Horatio's mother?" he said.

"Yes," she said.

"We have talked to several witnesses who tell us Horatio was estranged from Missus Huntington, that there were harsh words between them earlier today."

"I wouldn't know," she said. "I'm only his mother."

112

"Do you know where your son is?" Detective Strong said.

"No," Hunt's mother said.

"He seems to have disappeared," the detective said.

I stepped forward and said I had something to say. Detective Strong looked me up and down.

"You dress strangely, sir," he said. "Who are you?"

"I'm Evan Barksdale," I said. "I ... I was with Horatio drinking at the Bella Union for the last several hours, well, since the afternoon. I'm an old friend and mostly we just talked, catching up so to speak."

He jotted this information down in a notebook.

"Are you sure about the time?" the detective said.

"Absolutely," I said.

"Would you be willing to give a sworn statement to that effect?" he said.

"Yes," I said, and, trying to think quickly, added that I would be sailing on the next ship to the Orient.

"We won't detain you," he said.

Missus Huntington leaned toward me again.

"Thank god," she said. "I'm so relieved. So, who could have done it?"

Detective Strong had one of his men come over and take my sworn statement which he wrote down and then I signed it. After that I decided, out of curiosity, to step outside. Three horse and buggy carriages were lined up outside on the cobblestone street. I saw no sign of skyscrapers or any tall buildings. My heart raced at this whole incredible thing, that I was in fact somehow in another time, an era long past. Impossible, I thought. And yet, I was witness to this bizarre phenomenon, this quirk in time and space.

113

I went back inside and ran into Detective Strong, who was watching as they carried Gertrude out on a stretcher, covered with a shroud.

"Well, Mister Barksdale, have a wonderful journey to the Orient," he said.

"By the way," I said. "You might want to talk to Jason Margolo, rumors have it …"

"Yes, I know," Strong said. "We'll be catching up with him, soon enough."

I nodded and made my way back down through the lab to the underground portal where I expected Hunt to be waiting for me. He was not there. I was certain he had not come into the house. I decided to wait. I then found a note pinned to the door I hadn't seen before.

It said: *I went back to take care of that business at the house in 2021. Wait for me. You'll be pleased.*

I, of course, knew what he meant. About 40 minutes later he came bounding along, out of breath.

"I ran almost all the way back," he said. "How did it go with the police?"

"It's like time stood still all these years you were gone," I said. "But, my mission was successful. You are no longer a suspect."

"Good," Hunt said. "You've done well. I knew I could count on you."

"I put Detective Strong onto Jason Margolo also."

"Brilliant!" he said, then laughed uncontrollably for several seconds. "Of course, I did do it."

"Did what?"

"Poisoned Gertrude," he said, as if this should be no surprise. "She was a wretched creature, much like your Peggy I

114

imagine. So, I ground up some Strychnos plants from the Amazon and laced her tea with it. She threatened to leave with her lover and take our daughter. I wasn't going to have that."

"Your daughter?"

"Eleanor, Phoebe's mother," he said. "Enjoy my gift. It was the least I could do."

"What?" I said, uncertain.

"Goodbye, Evan. It's been grand."

He then disappeared into the shadows of the lab. I turned and made my way back to 2021, a journey I still really couldn't comprehend. I reached the space where I first encountered Hunt, then up the ladder into the turret. I closed the hatch and replaced the rug over it. Then up the second set of stairs and into the main body of the house. The moment I opened that door into the utility room I heard voices coming from upstairs. A woman was crying. There were a couple of uniformed police officers in the hallway.

"What's going on?" I said.

"You Mister Barksdale?" One of the officers said.

I nodded.

"There's been some trouble," he said. "Upstairs."

I went upstairs to find several more uniformed police officers and a couple of plain clothes detectives. I identified myself.

"Why are you here?" I said. "What's happened?"

Then I saw Cloe standing just inside the bedroom. She was the one I had heard crying. She turned and pointed a finger at me.

"Señor Barksdale did it," she said. "I heard him say he going to … get rid of his wife."

115

I was shown Peggy's body, naked in the bathtub, a knife plunged into her chest. It was gruesome. I recognized the knife as one from our kitchen. There was a note pinned to her by the knife. It read: "For you, Evan." Signed "Hunt."

Detectives Parnell and Conklin questioned me for over an hour about my whereabouts, and more importantly, who was Hunt? I told the whole story about finding Hunt in that room below the turret basement, about going back in time. They of course looked at each other like I was mentally off plumb.

"I know it sounds crazy," I said. "But, that's where I was when my wife was murdered, detectives. Hunt must have done it when I was back in 1882. He told me he'd left a surprise for me."

"Can you show us the room under the turret?" Detective Parnell said.

"Absolutely."

I led the way, to the utility room, through the door down to the bottom of the turret. They had flashlights and watched as I pulled back the rug to reveal the trap door. Only, there was no trap door. I searched every inch of that space under the rug, but there was no handle, no seams.

"This can't be," I said. "The trap door was here. I know it was here."

"You'll have to come with us, Mister Barksdale," Detective Parnell said.

I haven't spoken a word since that dark moment with the two detectives. I'm now sitting in a small room. Mostly, I stare into space. Someone feeds me from time to time. But what they don't know is I keep recounting my trip back in time. It's like watching a movie behind my eyes. It's all very clear. I can see Hunt. He's probably back where he belongs, telling friends in the Bella Union about his trip through time. About how he killed Peggy and craftily left my fingerprints on the knife. Since it was a kitchen knife my prints, of course, were on it. But why weren't his? Maybe he wore gloves. The point is, he thought I looked like Margolo and set me up. That's it!

An attendant told me I had a visitor. It was a tall dark man. He looked vaguely familiar. It was the strange cap with a feather in it that mostly jogged my memory.

"Alexander the Great," I mumbled.

He put his hands together.

"Namaste, Evan," he said. "Do you remember me? Aimilios. It's been many years. Your Aunt Phoebe's friend."

The woman attendant in a white uniform was nearby, watching, listening.

"Why am I in this place?" I said.

The tall dark man who called himself Aimilios, hesitated as if he were afraid to say the truth aloud.

"You're here instead of prison because your lawyer used the McNaughton Rule as your defense at the trial, over your objection. You don't remember? I was in the courtroom."

I slowly shook my head.

"What does that mean?"

"That you were, well … not in control of your faculties at the time of … the murder."

"Hunt did it," I said. "Horatio Huntington. He's the one with the demons! Not me. He's the man in the basement."

Aimilios did not react. Just looked at me, then nodded as if he understood.

"I've come to tell you I'll take care of the house until … well, until you get better."

117

Aimilios soon left. The woman attendant came over with a glass of something for me to drink. Thorazine, no doubt.

I looked up at her.

"Do you like children?" I said.

She looked at me and smiled.

"How are you today, Evan, or is it Hunt today? I never know which one I'm talking to."

I fought a smile trying hard to snake across my lips.

I don't know myself, I thought. It's a mysterious thing, an ambiguity of the cosmos. All I do know is Hunt is the reason I'm here. He's the man in the basement. And he won't leave.

Brenda Kahn

Disguise Artist

By Brenda Kahn

My father was a man of multiple disguises, although I didn't think of it in those terms when I was growing up in San Francisco. A fine artist by training who made his living as a graphic designer, he for a long time sported a goatee and mustache, completing the look with a beret perched on top of his head as if he had just stepped into San Francisco from the Montmartre artist quarter in Paris. His copper beard paired with his blue eyes also called to mind Van Gogh, as did his bouts of depression, although my dad managed to keep both ears. When he was painting in his basement studio, a cigarette or cigar would dangle from his lips — the accessory of artists everywhere, although in his case the cylinder of tobacco would be unlit, lest he set the house on fire by dropping an ember in the turpentine he used to clean his brushes.

My dad had a thing about tropical places — perhaps because they were the antithesis to the frozen landscape of Russia, where he spent his earliest years — and he loved anything having to do with the ocean and cruise ships, although he never learned how to swim. He cleverly worked out some kind of deal with Matson Lines, a leading cruise company at the time that docked its ocean liners in San Francisco, whereby he would get free or discounted family trips as part of his payment for graphic design services. He never explicitly admitted to a quid pro quo, but later on I figured out that this arrangement was the only way our middle-class, one wage-earner family of four could have afforded those exotic vacations to Honolulu and Acapulco. On board the ships, my dad was in his element, rocking a Hawaiian-style shirt every day, and holding court every night in the dining room, showing off his beautiful wife and two young daughters.

His collection of aloha shirts was vast, although I'm using the term broadly. Some were classically Hawaiian, sporting flowers and the like, while others were just cruise-style in design — button-down with an informal collar and short sleeves, and featuring synthetic material in colorful, geometric patterns. My dad's vacation wardrobe stood him in good stead later on, when he divorced my mother in his late 50s and moved as far away from California as he could, to the tip of Florida. Not only did he have four sisters to fall back on there, but also the hot and humid climate meant he could get away with wearing his island wardrobe most of the time.

At night in his modest one-bedroom Miami Beach bachelor apartment, he would take off the sweat-soaked shirts and rehang them in the closet instead of putting them in the dirty-clothes hamper, sensing that they were too fragile to wash with his underwear and the like, but not wanting to waste quarters on a special load of delicate laundry. There was also some magical thinking going on, in which he convinced himself that the damp garments would spontaneously self-deodorize and self-cleanse while hanging in the closet. On my visits to Florida every few months, I would wash his beloved Hawaiian shirts by hand, getting a great deal of satisfaction out of watching the water turn gray as the weeks of dried sweat dissolved.

On our family vacations, my dad would say *au revoir* to the beret, replacing it with one of his captain's hats, which he sought out in every port. In part, it was a statement of his affinity with everything tropical and nautical, and it also lent him an air of authority that his short stature often denied him. On the streets of Mexico, the storekeepers and restaurant workers would refer to him as *jefe,* or chief. On board the cruise ships, fellow passengers frequently took him for one of the senior crew members, which was just the way he wanted it. When he gave up married life and California, the captain's hats became part of his signature resort look as he navigated the streets of Miami Beach.

But it was on a trip to China post-divorce that my father picked up what perhaps was his most treasured article of clothing: an authentic version of a proletarian Mao jacket made out of thin, unlined navy blue fabric, with the trademark narrow collar, five buttons and a quartet of front pockets — two at the chest, two at the hips. In his later years, he rarely left his Miami Beach apartment without both his navy blue captain's hat and the matching Mao jacket. Not only was the jacket the perfect light topper for the always balmy Miami weather, but also it added to my father's mystique, marking him as a world traveler while simultaneously hinting at his days as a communist sympathizer.

My dad was as attached to the somewhat worn-out, fading garment as he was to any material object, so after he died in the year 2000 at the age of 86, I carried it back to the

Bay Area with me. To this day the jacket hangs in my coat closet, a reminder of everything endearing and enigmatic about my father.

My First Big Science Project

By Brenda Kahn

The instructions that Ari brought home from his second-grade teacher were simple enough. "Your child is to construct a solar system out of whatever materials he or she wants," she wrote. "You can advise them, but the child is to do it him- or herself." Attached was the teacher's drawing of one possibility, an array of paper planets suspended from a hanger. This easy way out was too simple for Ari, who declared that he wanted to make his solar system out of Styrofoam balls. I figured any 7-year-old who knew what Styrofoam was and could pronounce it correctly deserved to have it.

While I knew full well this was to be Ari's project, not mine, his skills at looking things up were nil. And since I was home on maternity leave with twin baby girls, I had more time than usual to make some calls in search of Styrofoam balls. After a couple hours of dialing five-and-dime stores and art supply stores, I struck gold at Ace Hardware on University Avenue in Berkeley. I headed there with the twins in tow, and walked out with about $50 worth of Styrofoam balls, pipe cleaners, glitter and paints. Driving up the bill was the necessity of buying double of everything so that Ari's little brother Zach wouldn't feel left out of the First Big Science Project.

Ari said he needed the glitter for the asteroid belt. I was quite impressed with his in-depth knowledge of the solar system. He knew the inner planets from the outer planets — although it was the first I'd heard of this two-tiered society in the solar system. He knew about the gas planets, and which ones have rings, visible and invisible. He knew which have moons, and which have orbits that cross, which have cloudy swirls, which are ice cold and which are red hot. Details that I had forgotten, or perhaps never learned in the first place.

We hit our first big snag about two minutes into the first phase of the project, which was decorating the planets with paint that, according to the label on the bottle, was "appropriate for any surface — wood, glass, plastic, etc." Apparently the only material it wouldn't stick to was Styrofoam. It beaded up into globs that refused to dry. The paint's saving grace was that it was fully washable, which is why I bought it in the first place. After about 10 minutes of this, with more paint on the kids' hands and clothes than on the balls, I called a halt to the operation. Luckily, the gooey stuff washed right off the balls, so at least our $25 investment in Styrofoam was salvaged.

The next day, the twins and I brought the paints back to the store. When I indignantly told the clerk that the paints misrepresented themselves, that they were not in fact good on any surface, he replied pleasantly, "Thank you. This is a new product and we need to know that kind of thing." Great, I thought to myself. At a time when the twins make any trip to the store a major expedition, I end up being the paint guinea pig. This time I headed for the heavy-duty permanent acrylics,

126

which specifically listed Styrofoam as a compatible surface. Downside: Once on clothes, furniture and the like, it never comes off.

A couple of days later, I got up my courage to launch back into phase one, planet painting. I warned Ari about my one rule: "Let me open the bottles of paint. Because if you try to do it, the paint is going to spurt all over, and this kind doesn't wash off."

Which Ari interpreted to mean, "Try your hand at unscrewing the lids." When I turned my back for a second, Ari grabbed a bottle, popped off the lid, ripped off the protective paper covering the opening and voila, brilliant orange spattered on our vintage teak dining room table, adjacent chairs, and the floor and wall. It missed the dining room curtains by just fractions of an inch. One blob landed on the car seat where one of the babies was sleeping, oblivious to the orange napalm that had just slimed her. It missed the top of her head by an inch or two — does acrylic paint wash out of hair, I wondered? I didn't want to find out. I was able to mop up most of the paint from the car seat, but it left an ugly three-inch stain that looked as though someone had spilled hot coffee on the baby.

Soon we were on to phase two, constructing rings. Although this came as news to me, not only does Saturn have rings, but so do Uranus, Neptune and Jupiter, per Ari. These he fashioned out of the pipe cleaners, although by the time he finished wrapping them around the toothpick supports jabbed into the planets, the rings were square instead of round. In a fit of enthusiasm and inspiration, Ari gave Jupiter a set of intersecting rings, so that the planet looked like a model of an atom, albeit one with square rings instead of round ones. He

127

seemed pleased with the results, so we went on to the next phase, namely depicting the planets' orbits.

I've never taken an engineering course, so I was operating on sheer guts and seat-of-the-pants instincts. Meanwhile, my husband Barrie, who is extremely mechanical and handy, had totally removed himself from the solar system project, and refused to offer any advice or physical assistance apart from providing some wire he had lying around, which we needed for the orbits.

We did okay with planets one and two, Mercury and Venus. Ari plunged a toothpick into the ball and threaded the wire, figuring out how big the orbit had to be to fit around our sun. But by the time we got to Earth, things were not going so well. The wider the concentric rings grew, the more the rather limp wire refused to lay flat or retain a circular form, instead springing back to the figure 8 shape it held before it was called into solar system service. What to do? Mom the wannabe engineer came to the rescue. I grabbed some bamboo cooking skewers and used them to support the rings and keep them properly spaced, securing everything with gold pipe cleaners whose sparkle I hoped would make up for the disorder of this celestial project.

"You're doing a good job making Ari's solar system," Barrie quipped during one of his walks by our growing catastrophe. By planet four, Ari declared that the model looked kind of weird.

"Noah and Yaeir are going to laugh at it," he said, referring to his two school buddies.

"No they're not. It's great — it's three dimensional," I retorted, feeling kind of defensive about my — I mean his — science project.

By now Ari had given up on struggling to make the wire flat long enough for him to measure and cut it, but I was in too deep to stop. So I carried on alone as he lay dejectedly on the living room bean bag. Somewhere around planet seven, Ari got a second wind, and jumped in for the finale. At this point I had worked out most of the engineering kinks, and we settled into a rhythm of cutting, looping and securing the wire orbits.

As the last step, Ari clipped the pointy skewer tips that were poking out too far, and we stepped back to admire our creation. In all, it was about 6 feet tall by about 4 feet wide, a monstrosity that resembled a spider web from a horror movie more than a solar system. On the bright side, while the sculpture was rather fragile and unwieldy, we didn't have to worry whether the ride to school would damage it, since the shape was rather organic to begin with. And there was little danger that the teacher would mark Ari's project down for excessive parental help — there was little evidence of that.

Kitchen Choreography

By Brenda Kahn

When my husband Barrie and I first bought our house in the Berkeley Hills, it had a lot of charming attributes, and one major failing: a miniscule kitchen, like something you might find in a trailer home or a food truck. In terms of layout, you could call it a truncated galley kitchen, featuring two counter areas facing off against each other, separated by a narrow aisle. Part of that already limited counter space is eaten away by the sink on one side, and the stovetop on the other, leaving just 9 linear feet of usable surface. Whereas the kitchen is often considered the heart of a home, in our abode it appears to be an afterthought.

While the house was designed by an architect, clearly he wasn't a foodie. Nor was he versed in feng shui. After living in the house for more than a decade, I learned to my horror that the placement of the stove directly opposite the sink was a recipe for disaster, with the fire element clashing with the water element and potentially causing family disharmony or worse. But nothing could be done about it then, apart from placing a goldfish tank on top of the backsplash separating the kitchen from the dining room, where the one and only

131

finned inhabitant could watch over the bustle in the kitchen and counteract the bad vibes with his shimmering orange presence (until Sparkle Rainbow grew to the size of a trout and had to be transported to a pond, but that's another story).

The core kitchen floor area measures 6.5 feet long by 4 feet wide, and in that small rectangle my husband Barrie and I have maneuvered for the last 30-plus years, preparing countless meals for our brood of four — often with a dog or kid or two underfoot, making the cramped space seem even tinier. We've taken liberties with the resources at hand, often turning the stovetop into a drying rack or a food prep area rather than let those 30 inches of flat surface go to waste. That we have managed to feed our family without suffering a catastrophic collision, burning ourselves or strangling each other in a fit of claustrophobia is a minor miracle.

But what is more impressive still is all the entertaining we've done from this dollhouse of a kitchen. Not just dinner parties for a few couples, but large events, from our two sons' circumcision celebrations to countless birthday parties, Thanksgiving meals for 16 or so family members, and Passover seders for 35 or more friends and relatives. We mostly make all the food from scratch, often spending hours of prep, cook and clean-up time in our micro kitchen together, standing shoulder to shoulder or butt to butt. I suppose it helps that we're both small people — with me clocking in at 5 feet 2 inches, and Barrie just a tad taller, neither one of us takes up that much space. More than that, though, it's the choreography that makes it all work.

While Barrie and I are often at loggerheads about many things around the house — what temperature the thermostat should be set at, or whether the lights in temporarily vacated rooms should be turned off, to name just a couple flashpoints — the tight quarters of the kitchen require absolute and unquestioning cooperation, especially when the clock is ticking and guests are due to arrive shortly. On such occasions, our slow-simmering marital disputes are put aside as our bodies glide past each other with just an inch or two to spare, and as one pair of hands reaches over, under or around the other's, gracefully and wordlessly, seemingly guided by an invisible air traffic controller. Over time our reflexes and peripheral vision have sharpened, so that if I dare to reach across Barrie's cutting board to access the faucet while he's wielding a 10-inch chopping knife, his blade pauses in midair instinctively until my hand retracts, without any utterances of "excuse me" or "sorry" necessary between us.

Somehow we've avoided stabbing each other as we've sliced and diced our way through king-sized bowls of tabouli (courtesy of Molly Katzen's *Moosewood Cookbook*), green salads galore with Barrie's trademark balsamic dressing (the secret is in the fenugreek) and poached salmon with yogurt-cucumber sauce (the only thing I make from Martha Stewart's *Entertaining* cookbook). For Passover, Barrie cooks up huge pots of matzoh ball soup, while I experiment with various recipes for gefilte fish, an old-world delicacy that is an acquired taste, but nonetheless is an essential part of the tradition.

Lacking such commonplace amenities as a food-prep island, a second oven, a six-burner stovetop or an overflow garage refrigerator (the latter being impossible since we don't have a garage to put it in), we've had to improvise. Sometimes food prep spills over to the dining room table, and when we need extra refrigerator space, our next-door neighbors have been generous with theirs. We calculate the cooking time needed for the various dishes, and artfully allocate scarce burner and oven rack space accordingly.

But now, after three-plus decades of hands large and small mauling our cabinets and six pairs of feet (eight if you count the dog's four legs) pounding the floor, the kitchen is overdue for an overhaul. The wood veneers on the cabinet doors are peeling, while the funky reddish granite countertops and coordinating tile floor look hopelessly outdated. Moreover, the appliances are simultaneously coming to the end of their lives. The refrigerator has been on its last legs for years (alternating between alarming warming periods and freezing all the produce), the dishwasher seems to deposit more dirt than it removes and the glass stovetop is cracked like an iPhone screen.

The only question is, does it pay to enlarge the kitchen while we're at it, or should we keep the original footprint? Our next-door neighbor Ron, an architect and foodie, considers our tiny kitchen unworkable, and has been encouraging us to knock out a wall so as to capture the space in the adjoining entryway (although perhaps this recommendation is driven in part by his annoyance with our excess cold stuff overflowing into his refrigerator every time we have a big party). His scheme might even allow for my longed-for food-prep island — albeit at a significant extra cost.

Part of me wonders whether it makes sense to spend that kind of money on enlarging our kitchen at a time when our kids are mostly launched and on the road to creating families and holiday traditions of their own. But I also hesitate to alter the carefully calibrated recipe that has bound Barrie and me together all these years. The prospect of expanding our kitchen brings to mind the cautionary tale of my college boyfriend's family. They built an expansive custom home in the lush green hills of a Bay Area suburb, and the sudden abundance of interior space and the ability to avoid close, continual contact with each other accelerated the family's unraveling into a messy divorce.

In our case, I wonder if it's the constant friction in the kitchen that keeps Barrie and me Velcroed to one another, the churning of the mixing paddles of all the food-centered holidays and celebrations sweeping us up into a marriage goulash that somehow works because of the tight space, not in spite of it.

In the Shower With Grandma

By Brenda Kahn

I use the same technique for bathing Grandma as I do for our dog, Chance, although she would hate that comparison because she dislikes all dogs in general, and our boxer in particular. The only difference is that Chance is considerably more cooperative and less *kvetchy* — a Yiddish word that means a tendency to complain a lot about nothing.

When I want to bathe Chance, I say, "Chance, let's take a bath," and he obediently goes to the bathroom and gracefully maneuvers his 65 pounds into the tub, and waits for me to turn on the water. I then wet him down with the detachable shower head, scrub him from nose to tail and rinse, shielding his eyes from the spray.

It takes only three towels to bathe and dry Chance. It takes at least seven towels for Grandma's shower — one to place on the toilet seat top so her bare, bony bottom won't be cold while she sits there to undress and dress, one to place on the folding chair I put in the shower so she can sit while I wash her, two to place on the floor to keep her feet warm, two to dry her body, and another small one to dry her face. A whole washer load of towels per shower.

Whenever Grandma visits our house in Berkeley, I ask, "Do you want to take a shower?" and then ensues the script where she tells me it is too cold, and I reassure her that I will crank up the heat in the bathroom. I persist because her independent living facility across the bridge in Marin County doesn't offer help with bathing, and I am the only family member not squeamish about looking at her naked or washing all her body parts. "The people at the home can't believe my daughter-in-law gives me a shower," she has told me more than once. No one would guess that I have the routine down because I've had lots of practice with the dog.

I have never called my mother-in-law "Mom," which perhaps is mean of me, but I can't help it. At first I called her Esther, and once the kids were born, I added Grandma to the mix. I have loved her for these past 30 years, and am eternally grateful that each time I gave birth (three deliveries resulting in four kids), she came up to Berkeley from Southern California to help. She was the ultimate Jewish mother, in the good sense of the term, baking kugels and roasting briskets, and doing whatever else needed to be done the first couple of weeks after the births, uncomplainingly.

When she was more mobile, my mother-in-law was my favorite shopping buddy, in part because we shared a fondness for animal prints and things that sparkle. I considered her my good luck charm because I always found something great on sale when I trolled Macy's or Nordstrom's with her. But I never considered her to be my second mother. Maybe it's because I lost my own mother just three months before I met my husband, and by the time we got married a year later, my mother had been dead only 15 months. It was all too raw and painful to be thinking of calling someone else "Mom" so quickly. My mother-in-law accepted my calling her Esther and Grandma, and I am grateful for that as well.

It takes Grandma several minutes to shuffle to the bathroom, a solid 15 seconds to sit down on top of the closed toilet. Each shift is a study in slow motion, and she sighs, pauses and grunts with every move. I try to dial down my metabolism and turn up my patience level, but at a certain point I step in to speed things up. I help her lift her sweater over her head, and remove the pull-on bra that is stuffed on one side with a silicone prosthesis. Now that I've seen her naked so many times, it seems perfectly natural that one side of her chest is completely flat, while the other sports a pendulous breast that is strangely smooth, full and youthful-looking compared to the rest of her 93-year-old face and body. My mother-in-law has always been well endowed, her generous cup size out of sync with a body that has always been svelte and petite, and now has shriveled to 90 pounds, if that.

At first it seemed indelicate to touch the one breast, which hangs to her waist, and I would say, "Esther, can you lift your boob?" But she's too hard of hearing to understand what I'm saying, especially with the water running and her hearing aids removed, so now I delicately lift the pinkish orb to wash, rinse and dry the skin underneath. And in a funny way, it's tit for tit. When my first son was born, he was slow to nurse, perhaps being too drugged up from my epidural to bother. Per the lactation consultant's advice, Esther got in bed with me, and patiently used an eyedropper to drip formula on my nipple to entice him to latch on. I quickly got over the embarrassment of my mother-in-law looking at my naked breast, just as she now has had to get over the embarrassment of her daughter-in-law looking at hers.

As I start to unbuckle her shoes and remove her knee-high stockings, she protests with "I can do it." But she can't, and I wonder how she manages to get dressed and undressed when I'm not around, which is most of the time. On one of her recent sleepovers at our house in Berkeley, I discovered that she had crawled into bed fully clothed. "Esther, you need to get undressed," I admonished her. "Why bother?" she resisted. "I just have to get dressed again in the morning."

With both the wall heater and the space heater going at once, and the hot water running at full blast, the bathroom feels like a steamy Bikram yoga studio, and I pull off my own top to mitigate the heat. Now naked and standing by the side of the tub, Esther pauses to thrust one of her shaky hands into the stream of water and declares, "It's too cold," although it is as hot as her thin skin can tolerate. She looks around for something to grab onto, not trusting my helping hand, and reaches for the water faucet handle. "Esther, don't grab the faucet — you'll burn yourself," I warn her.

Finally, she is seated on the folding chair in the tub, and the scrubdown begins. When I ask her to stand so I can reach her private parts, she again reaches for the faucet handle to balance herself. Both of my hands are busy at the moment — with one holding her up while the other aims the detachable shower head at her body — so I yell, "No, don't touch the faucet!"

My mother-in-law's steep downhill slide started about two years ago, when she totaled her Camry while cruising down a boulevard in Huntington Beach. At the age of 91 she was an accident waiting to happen, seeing as how she had shrunk to the point where she could barely see over the

140

steering wheel, couldn't hear ambient noises that give drivers clues as to what's going on around them and lacked the reflexes to react quickly. She was lucky to come out of the accident alive, albeit with a cracked pelvis and damage to various soft tissues. After a month or so in the hospital and a nursing facility, she recovered enough to move up to Northern California to be near her kids and grandchildren. Still, the trauma took a lot out of her, and she is a shadow of her former self, unsteady on her feet and prone to falls. And the sweet Jewish mother persona has melted away, leaving behind a caricature of a cantankerous, hard-to-please and sometimes belligerent elder.

The crankiness is mostly reserved for other family members, with her most vicious outbursts directed at our dog, Chance. "Get away from me," she barks at him whenever he approaches, and he freezes, his soulful eyes looking fearful and silently asking why anyone would hate his sweet presence so. For some reason, my mother-in-law keeps her orneriness in check around me, and for that I am grateful.

Just as shopping used to be our thing, now showers are what bind us. This week, I add a new element: washing and setting her hair. I twist her thin strands of silvery white hair onto foam curlers, then rig up an old-fashioned bonnet dryer by covering the haphazard mess of curlers with a shower cap and filling it with hot air from a blow dryer. When I comb her hair out, she almost looks like her old self, well-groomed and put together.

After we are all done with the washing, the drying, the rubbing down with lotion, the dressing and the hair curling, she says, "There are no words for what you are doing."

"Is that a good thing or a bad thing?" I ask, half joking, half not. She doesn't answer.

Time in a Jar

By Brenda Kahn

As is the case with many people, the Covid-19 crisis and forced sequestering at home produced in me a syndrome not yet recognized by the CDC: the urge to tidy up cabinets and closets that have been languishing in chaos for decades. At a time when most aspects of everyday life — from going to restaurants and shopping for groceries to visiting with friends and family — were suddenly severely restricted or drastically morphing, I found the vetting and organizing process oddly calming and cathartic.

First I organized the spice drawer, cleaning out an accumulation of aromatic debris and alphabetizing the slender jars for the first time in the 30-plus years we've lived in our Berkeley home. Then it was on to weeding through the jumble of the hallway linen closet, tossing single sheets that had mysteriously lost their mates and donating my adult kids' childhood twin sheet sets to a friend who was making Covid masks. Next I tackled the kitchen cabinet housing storage containers, discarding orphaned tops that didn't match any bottoms, and bottoms whose lids seemingly had been swallowed whole by the dishwasher.

I saved the biggest challenge for last: the pantry, a narrow cabinet to the left of the refrigerator, which I tackled about three months into the lockdown. To my credit, I had maintained some semblance of organized chaos here over the years, with one shelf set aside for canned goods, the next one down reserved for anything that comes in a bottle or jar, and the next two stuffed with grains, flour and other dry goods.

We've kept the can shelf relatively up to date, every winter weeding out the items approaching their expiration dates and donating them to holiday food drives. But since you can't donate anything contained in glass, the jar shelf had become a black hole, with everyday items like mustard, mayo and capers mixed in with more adventurous bruschetta dips and tapenades, and mystery condiments. Some were homemade holiday gifts or souvenirs from our friends' and relatives' travels, while others were impulse purchases at Trader Joe's, purveyor of exotic food items from around the globe at bargain basement prices.

There was a jar of strawberry, peach and prosecco jam, compliments of Joan and Bob's Juicy Jams in Kilkenny, Ireland — is Ireland known for its jams, I wondered? And what's Italian prosecco got to do with it? But since there were a couple more months until the expiration date, I didn't have the heart to toss it. Another cultural mishmash was the *artischoken caponata*, produced in Italy for a German company — also with an impending end date.

Then there were the expired items in various stages of decay, with "best by" dates going back to 2014, 2007 and beyond. The most ancient by far were two squat jars of Trader Joe's muffuletta spread — a tapenade mix on steroids — with expiration dates in the year 2000. I immediately got nostalgic for that more innocent era two decades prior, before 9/11 changed everything in the external world, and, a year or so before that catastrophe, my father's death upended my internal world.

But the pangs of nostalgia quickly gave way to curiosity. From the outside, the colors of the chopped-up black and green olives, mixed with flecks of red pepper, still seemed vibrant. If a jar stays sealed and intact for two decades, are the contents technically safe to eat? I was torn. On the one hand, it would be ironic to die of self-induced food poisoning after surviving months of the Covid-19 pandemic threat. Then again, how could I toss not one, but two jars of what could be perfectly good muffuletta spread without giving it a try?

I called over my husband Barrie, who is far less discerning when it comes to food expiration dates, and has been known to eat from a Costco roasted chicken for three weeks — two weeks longer than I would, back when I was still eating meat.

"Would you eat this if it's from 2000?"

"Open it up and smell it," he advised.

And so we did. I expected to get a pungent whiff of something putrid, like a tin of that notorious fermented Swedish herring that is best opened from the rear of a fast-moving boat. But instead, we smelled nothing. Perhaps it was so old that it had lost its punch, I hypothesized. I called my neighbor Ron, a master chef who usually has an answer for any kitchen quandary.

"Would you eat a jar of something from 2000?" I asked.

"If you try it first," he said, laughing.

Barrie was game, but then I fast forwarded in my mind to the scene in the ER, where I would have to admit that I had poisoned my husband with 20-year-old muffuletta, and perhaps face attempted manslaughter charges. So, reluctantly, I emptied both jars into the food scraps tub, and said goodbye to the year 2000 for the second time.

Edie Meidav

Another Love Discourse

Excerpts From a Lyric Novel
By Edie Meidav

Atopos

By Edie Meidav

> Here, back east,
> I keep seeing wrong
> things in the right places, howling
> faces everywhere but
> especially in the upturned
> roots: great fallen trees,
> guts entombed in mud.

There is no change of death in Paradise, says Wallace, enshrined in Hartford, one hour south of where I usually live in the newish parsonage, but he might as well have been schrying California.

Might as well have said *there is no change of Paradise in death:* your horizon of hope after a beloved dies may not alter.

A kind of epic without the heroic, Roland says of Maman, mourning her lifelong struggles, and also: *what I find terrifying is mourning's discontinuity.* Rupture of a rupture: who loves that?

149

What becomes a binary best: do we most trust what stays?

Or do we least trust what might rupture?

What if we only know how to trust when ruptured?

The whole time I grip onto the ideal of motherhood
it seems to be happening without
my noticing, around me, in the cracks.

Anxiety

By Edie Meidav

Roland's mother, cast out of her own mother's fancy family, makes do in the bosom of the less cultured family of her late husband. Young Roland clings to her: large, at the age where he is *meant to be* standing alone.

What would Donald Winnicott say? Henrietta was more than a good-enough mother. Present if querulous. As Roland says, days after her death: *I keep hearing her voice telling me to wear a little color.*

Meant to be: a young man standing on spindly legs facing the photographer. Instead, he clings, watchful, big for his shorts, the distance between the two mandated. The question remains: would he suckle if he could?

Wouldn't anyone? Middle daughter says she cannot help the jealousy, seeing me hold someone's flirtatious baby: *I miss that belonging to you,* she says, *I want to be a baby all over.* Knowing herself that much.

Later I intone, pedantic: all war comes from the same wish —
if not to suckle then to belong! Everyone covers the wish to
belong and connect. They feel hurt and over that lay in the
mud of righteousness, uproar, spleen, identity, tribalism, the
martial.

You should be a daily influencer, she says, *I subscribe to stuff like
that, it helps me survive, I'd subscribe to you,* and in what she says I
flush with belonging, feeling I belong not just to her but to
the umbilicus of outermost signs, the screen a transitional
object, that I might yet become the motherscreen she thumbs
and believes.

After the photo, Roland goes on to live with mother on and
off for some fifty years, seeing her struggles as noble. Friends
and foes will call him an avid, rapacious guest at their dinner
parties, a man eternally legislating the discord between body
and mind, on diet plans meant to contain the wish: to suckle
more than he needs. His body continues the great betrayal
begun in adolescence: at the sanatorium instead of college,
breathing afresh an institution's order, its community and
meals. Hypervigilant and frail within traitorous body, he micro-
analyzes what happens on the surface of villi and skin, attends
costume galas in broad swashbuckling drag.

Chère Maman cheers from the sidelines, and back home, he
makes up for lost time, lives with her. For a half-century! (She
dies.) A handful of months beyond her death, in a fug, he is
hit by a laundry truck and soon follows that originating body,
mother, tunnels down toward her, and will no longer be
betrayed by the waxwork of physical self, the question worn

by coming out of her. He melts back toward the woman who offered him resentment, whose worth he believed had never been fully understood, high-born but treated wrongly by her own motherroot. Having explicated the worth of the individual and her choices, the slippery code of the self as it struggled to communicate such worth to anyone who would understand. A boy born second year of the first world war in the same era that one poet declaimed *the center could not hold* and another called out to a chorus of angels and asked could anyone hear? The world falling apart birthed the question: what private voice can be heard and understood? Forget mother — might understanding itself become a lover, with unmothering only the background, a world-echo?

Jeanne B. Perkins

Our Australian Outback Huntsman

By Jeanne B. Perkins

The Red Center of the Outback has huntsmen — not the kind that shoot critters, but the kind that make you want to shoot them, if you didn't think they'd jump up and fight back.

These huntsmen LOVE cars. Hertz ought to warn us unsuspecting tourists when they hand over the keys to rental vehicles.

It might have taken us a bit longer to meet our personal huntsman if we were not used to driving on the right-hand side of the road with the steering wheel on the left. Because Australia was an English colony, the Aussies drive on the left with the steering wheel on the right. The first time my husband Dale signaled for a turn in our rental car in Alice Springs, he grabbed the lever on the left side of the steering wheel out of habit. Instead of the blinker, he got the windshield wipers, disrupting the midday nap of the resident huntsman. Needless to say, our 4-inch diameter huntsman scampered out of bed and up the windshield. Gasping, Dale did his best to not drive off the road as the huge spider darted around inches away.

Huntsman spiders love the Outback, and they particularly love car dashboards and windshield wiper recesses.

Luckily, the resident huntsman in our car was living in the windshield wiper recess — and thus crawled out onto the OUTSIDE of the window. (They also love to live in curtains. It is noteworthy that our apartment did not have curtains, or I might have found a different place to spend the night.) It is also lucky that the huntsman spider that lived in our car was not fully grown, for apparently they grow to be the size of a plate.

The huntsman spider made Australian Geographic magazine's list of Australia's 10 most dangerous spiders (August 2012). Huntsman spiders are "reluctant to bite and more likely to run away when approached and their venom isn't considered dangerous for humans. Their danger comes more from causing accidents by the terrified drivers who react to a huntsman jumping out from behind the sun visor or dashboard of a car when it's in motion."

Later in the day, Dale and our college-aged son Kevin hopped back in the car to drive to get take-out kebabs for dinner, this time with Kevin in the front passenger seat. (There was NO WAY that I was going to get back in that car with the huntsman still living there.) It didn't take Dale long to accidentally start the wipers as he tried to signal a turn, once again disturbing our huntsman. This time Kevin got a close-up view of the spider as it scampered up the windshield to the top of the car. Stopping, they were reluctant to exit the car with a spider on the roof, but on the count of 1-2-3, they simultaneously bailed out. Kevin grabbed a long stick and swished him off, at which point they quickly hopped back in the car and zoomed off, half expecting to see the huntsman's 8-inch-diameter mother chasing them! I'm certain Dale didn't pay Kevin enough for this act of heroism.

In retrospect, it's amazing that our huntsman encounter was more memorable than our encounters with the wallabies and kangaroos — or even with the crocodiles — on our vacation!

Off-Road Obsessions

By Jeanne B. Perkins

I head into my garage one morning about six months after the COVID pandemic hit when it happens — I hear my 2006 red Subaru Forester in a heated argument with my husband Don's 2004 white Toyota Sienna minivan. After regaining my senses, I ask the Forester, "WHAT in Heaven's name is going on here?"

My red car replies, "You've been in lockdown. I've been in lockdown. And my minivan lockdown mate here, Mack, is a top-rate jerk."

That's when I remember that my Forester admitted he could talk about two years ago. But in the meantime, I had decided that I must have just hallucinated it and forgotten about it. I just stare at both of them.

"Hey, Julie," the Subaru continues. "You remember, right? I'm your buddy Roger."

"Just vaguely," I reply. "You have to admit that we haven't driven either of you two vehicles much in several months — mostly using our bicycles and having everything delivered."

"That's just the problem. I haven't left the garage in five months — and that snot-rag Mack beside me has been out with Don at least once a week."

"Don uses him to get our drive-up-and-go groceries."

"Will I ever get out of this garage jail?"

I smile. "Since we're getting ready to leave on a road trip to the desert in a couple of days, I thought I should check on you. We've decided we're taking you camping!"

At that moment, Roger starts gasping for air as he mumbles, "I thought you'd forgotten about me."

I become both puzzled and concerned. "What on earth is the problem?"

Roger gives one final gasp as he mumbles, "I think my battery is dying!"

At this point, my husband Don has heard the ruckus and wanders into the garage to find the battery charger in a corner full of cobwebs. "Roger, let's see if we can recharge it for you!"

Looking at my car, all I can say is, "It looks like he is on life support, poor guy."

"He's a car — not a person — even though he still continues to talk too much. He'll be fine."

The next morning, we head into the garage to check on Roger. I am shocked, "He looks AWFUL."

Don climbs in and turns the key. "Nothing. He can't even begin to start."

I can't stand it and pat my car buddy on his hood. "Don will get you fixed. I hope you can hear me."

Don opens the hood and extracts the battery. Grabbing his best COVID mask, he explains, "It looks like I need to head to Costco with the old battery and exchange it for a new one."

That afternoon, he returns, opens the hood and installs his new purchase. "There! That should make Roger reliable enough to take us on a trip with no Wi-Fi, no cell service and almost no people!"

Roger wakes up, quite excited. He waggles his tires and starts to skitter back and forth in the garage. "I feel like a teenager going off to my first co-ed party!"

I shake my head in disbelief and pat him on his hood. "Keep calm. I know you blame Don for 'abandoning' you and always taking the minivan during COVID, but we haven't gone far from home — and definitely haven't spent the night in those places."

Roger looks surprised. "So you will be sleeping with me? I don't know if I can fit both you and Don. Perhaps Don could sleep outside?"

Don groans. "NO ONE is sleeping with you."

I grin. "Don't you remember what a nightmare of a time I had trying to camp with you? I didn't take a tent and discovered that I could barely extract myself through a partially blocked side door once I closed myself in!"

"But you could easily climb in through my hatchback!"

"I was able to easily climb IN through your hatchback — but because the hatchback does not have an inside handle, I had to extract myself by doing a contorted limbo move out one of your side doors. NO WAY am I sleeping in you again!"

The next morning, Don and I pack Roger full of our camping supplies and food for a week before loading our two bicycles on the back.

Roger looks shocked. "I've never been so stuffed! Are you sure there are just two of you?"

Calmly, I reply, "We're heading to the desert. We even need to take our own water. We're staying at Jumbo Rocks in Joshua Tree National Park but there is no water at the campsite, just at the visitor center 30 minutes away."

At the end of a LONG drive, we arrive at our campsite. Roger looks disgusted. "Where's the dirt? We've been on pavement all day!"

Don replies, "You have no patience!"

I continue, "Roger, just be patient. We're going to fix dinner and explore this area. Then tomorrow morning we'll …"

Roger beeps his horn in disgust. "You're leaving me at this campground? Where are you two headed?"

I sound a bit apologetic. "The sun has almost set and it's finally getting cool. We're off on a hike. We'll be taking a hike most mornings and evenings — but in the middle of the day in the midday sun, we'll take you on some fun dirt."

Roger isn't buying it. "Promise?"

"Promise! We'll need your air conditioning!"

The next morning as we are cleaning up after breakfast, Roger looks ready to explode. "I bet you're off on ANOTHER hike. I've been double-crossed! This campground is BORING. You TRICKED me and I am certain that Don is behind it! That's deceitful!"

"Nope. Not this morning," I reply. "We're taking you on a drive to the far west side of the park, so we need to leave a bit early. We want to get to the summit of Eureka Peak at 11 a.m."

"FINALLY — some dirt, right?"

"It's technically a four-wheel-drive road, but you may be a bit disappointed. The last time we drove to the summit we were in a two-wheel-drive rental car."

As we drive to the start of our adventure, Roger loses patience. "This is nothing but asphalt. I want DIRT!"

But Don is excited. "I am SO looking forward to tackling Eureka Peak! Let me out here and I'll ride my bike to the summit!"

Shortly after Don starts his ride, I make a left turn and Roger slides around as we hit some deep sand. He looks puzzled. "This isn't dirt — it's something different. Is it SNOW?"

I explain. "It's sand. And a lot of it! This is mapped as an easy section of road that is supposed to be two-wheel-drive. I'm glad I'm driving you, not our minivan!"

"Me too! This is fun! There's more of those weird trees. They look deformed!"

"They're called Joshua trees, even though they're not actually trees, but rather a type of yucca. Their common name 'Joshua tree' was given to them by a group of Mormon settlers in the mid-1800s who imagined these trees raising their arms to pray, much like in the biblical story of Joshua."

"If you say so. I still maintain that the trees are WEIRD. Is Don still trying to ride his bicycle in this sand?"

"I gave him this trip to the desert as part of his Christmas present, telling him he would have fun riding his mountain bike here."

"But he's stopped already — and looks grumpy!"

Don loads his bike back on Roger. "I can't ride in this sand without wider tires. It's TOO deep. This 'present' you gave me seems like an excuse to have company while YOU take Roger to the desert."

I try to keep everyone calm. "The road will improve as it heads uphill. They always do!"

Two minutes later, Don announces, "Amazing. The road is better already. Let me try to ride again! Plus, if I'm on my bike, I don't have to listen to Roger complain."

It takes Roger, Don and I two hours to reach the summit. I leap out of the car to run and hug Don. "You did it! You need to pose with your bike over your head! You conquered Eureka Peak."

Roger sputters grumpily, "Give me some credit. I conquered it as well!"

I manage to ignore the car as I continue to talk with Don. "And the crazy part is that once the Park Service map decreed that the road was four-wheel-drive only, it immediately improved!"

Roger butts in. "That's because the sand disappeared. I was having fun in that lower section."

Don climbs back in the car as I announce, "Let's take the LONG way back to our campsite via Cap Rock!"

Roger is mystified. "A ROCK is wearing a baseball cap? Is it worried about sunburn?"

I ignore him and continue. "That's just its name. It's a big rock with a little rock that sits on its top, a bit tilted. Somebody thought that it looked like a cap."

"Stupid if you ask me."

I continue. "All the major rocks here have names: Skull Rock, Face Rock, Split Rock, Arch Rock — and a group of rocks called the Hall of Horrors."

166

But Roger has more questions. "When will I get more dirt?"

I am exasperated. "Jesus! Have some patience. We're turning left here. This is where Don probably wants to ride his bike. Let's let him out."

Don announces, "OK Roger, take care of Julie. See you both at Cap Rock." He likely would be losing patience too if he hadn't been able to ride his bike.

Again, I find myself explaining things to Roger. "We'll follow Don through Queen Valley — and then pick him up at Cap Rock."

An hour later, Roger has already started to complain again. "This is some of the smoothest 'dirt' I've ever driven. Mack the Minivan could do this road easily. I want REAL dirt."

"Yes, but it's great for Don to bicycle on. You will get some real dirt. Probably tomorrow."

"I know — patience — patience — patience."

"You keep complaining and saying you want DIRT. But is that true? You seem really uptight."

"I just want to be able to brag to that idiot minivan of Don's that I went on roads that vain busy-body couldn't handle."

"Is that all? Are you sure that's it?"

"Look — I like you and I want you to like me. Just appreciate me because, just as you do, I LIKE dirt."

An hour later Roger and I arrive at our destination. I grin. "Here's Cap Rock! And there's Don. See, that wasn't so bad."

"Not bad — but not good either."

The next morning, we drive to the Pinto Basin, where two separate dirt roads head into the distance, one called Old Dale Road, and a second called Black Eagle Mine Road. Don looks concerned. "I checked these out on the internet. Both look nasty. That's why I left my bicycle back at our campsite."

Roger acts the opposite. "PERFECT. I am SO excited! Sounds like REAL dirt today!"

I chime in. "I know very little about either option, except that we are unlikely to make it to the end of either road. We'll just go a while, and then turn around when things look sketchy."

Roger immediately has to butt into our conversion. "Hey! What do you think I am? Certainly not a prissy Porsche or a vain minivan. I'm TOUGH!"

Don has to correct him. "But you aren't a Jeep either. Let's just take this one step at a time."

"If you say so. But I have to warn you. I don't have much patience."

Don grins. "That's certainly an understatement. Let's explore Black Eagle Mine Road first."

Fifteen minutes later Roger starts complaining again. "This first part is no harder than Queen Valley was yesterday. BORING!"

I agree. "You're right. This flat part across the Pinto Basin is pretty dull. Hey — that looks like an old mine and there's one on the left as well."

"Just like you two. Leave me by the side of the road so you can go off looking at ROCKS. Don't you get it? Rocks are rocks — NOT dirt!"

I climb back in the car to show Don the rock I just found. "Check out this blue rock. That must have been an area where they processed copper ore."

Roger smirks. "Looks like any other rock to me. Gray."

"Let me explain," I continue. "That blue shimmer is typical of copper ore. But this doesn't have much — likely the stuff they threw out as worthless. Next stop — those mountains ahead!"

As we approach the mountains, Roger slows down and refuses to speed ahead. "This is no longer dirt at all — just rock slabs! I might damage my undercarriage!"

I ignore him. "Let's get out, Don, and check out the scenery!"

Just as we close the doors, Roger begins to slide. "HELP! You forgot to set the emergency brake!"

Don races to open the Subaru's passenger door. "I can barely reach the hand brake."

I start screaming. "Be careful or you both will end up heading over that cliff!"

Don continues, "It's not strong enough to stop the car from running off the road!"

Roger suddenly begins to whimper. "HELP! You two are about to kill me! I'm not ready to die!"

That's when I have an idea. "I can jump in the driver's seat and steer Roger away from the edge!"

I manage to turn the wheel to head the car away from the cliff and uphill so the brakes can hold. It works. Roger is still shaken up and remarkably quiet as we drive back to our campground.

Don can't resist teasing Roger, "So I thought that you were TOUGH, not a prissy Porsche."

Roger sputters in disgust but keeps heading forward.

After about an hour, we are climbing up a small rise before our final descent into the area of our campground when Don sounds the alarm. "I don't want to scare anyone, but this temperature gauge shows that Roger is getting overheated."

"Probably due to too much complaining," I joke.

Don becomes more insistent. "I think we should pull over and see if Roger cools down on his own."

Pulling over, we climb out and walk down an interesting wash to allow the car to cool off. But climbing back in and starting Roger up again, we see the gauge is still in the red. I shake my head. "We need to come up with a Plan B."

After searching through all our gear, we find a gallon jug of water. Don carefully loosens the radiator cap, only to see steam shoot five feet into the air. We wait another 10 minutes before being able to add water.

I have limited cell phone coverage but determine that there is a car repair shop in the small town just to the north of the park — 20 miles away. "What do you think?"

Don is more proactive. He props up Roger's hood and is looking hopefully as a couple of cars pass before a Jeep pulls up next to us. The owner asks, "Need help?"

"Some spare water would be great!" Between that Jeep and a second one that stops shortly thereafter, we manage to feed Roger a gallon of cold water and keep two more for our trip.

Roger has been abnormally silent. I think being overheated is affecting his brain. But soon the cold water kicks in and he begins to rant. "I'm so HOT. I've got a terrible fever! I think I caught COVID."

"Cars don't get COVID," I reply calmly.

"But cats do," Roger continues to rant. "That black cat next door must have climbed under my hood and sneezed and given it to me! I can't smell or taste anything!"

I shake my head and reply, "You've never been able to smell or taste."

We decide to ignore him and drive five miles before stopping again to let him cool off and feed him one more gallon of water. That's when the ranting begins again. "You should have vaccinated me months ago. I'm over 12 years old — so I'm eligible."

"Look," I reply, "CARS can't get COVID. Something else is going on."

Again, we drive another five miles before stopping to let him cool off and feed him our last gallon of cold water. All of us are silent as we drive into town to Mercy Repair Clinic. We feed Roger yet more water from the shop's faucet and are waiting for one of the mechanics to check Roger out when the car has another demand. "I want monoclonal antifreeze! You can't let me die from this!"

We talk to the shop owner, determine that Roger likely needs a new water pump, and agree to return the next day. It's a hot bicycle ride back to our campground — and a bit weird to be "car camping" without a car.

Returning to Mercy the next day, we find out that the heater hose had sprung a leak and needed to be replaced, not the water pump. But Roger is still convinced he recovered because of monoclonal antifreeze (even though he got nothing but plain water).

As we head home, Don tries to be patient. "I know you think I'm a jerk, but I did get you fixed twice in the past week — first with a new battery and now a new hose."

Roger starts thinking again. "THAT's something I can brag to Mack the Minivan about!"

The Case of the Hounds of Botallack

By Jeanne B. Perkins

I usually get up quite late in the morning, except when I get involved in some research project or another and end up staying up all night perfecting mathematical models of genetic diseases. I suppose it was lucky that last night was one of those nights, for I was seated having my breakfast — yogurt and granola with lots of extra nuts and craisins, and a bit of hot chocolate with whipped cream — when someone had the audacity to ring my doorbell.

I pulled my sweatshirt over my head to appear somewhat respectable at what I view as the ungodly early hour of 9 a.m. and opened the door.

Before me stood a young woman — exceedingly tall and thin. (Actually, she was tall and thin like a model, and I must admit I was jealous. I am a bit overweight, and am forever dreaming of being "tall and thin.") In her hand she was carrying a walking stick. As I looked at it, I noticed that under its head was a broad silver band nearly an inch across. She raised it so I could better read: "To James Mortimer, M.R.C.S., from his friends of the C.C.H., 1884." I squirmed, for I knew from family lore that this must be THE walking stick that belonged to THE James Mortimer, my famous great-great-uncle's one-time client.

She slumped into my living room, wearing a wool coat and shivering, even though it was during summer and already quite warm. "May I sit?"

I laughed as I replied, "Of course! Even though you appear in your mid-30s, you look like you might collapse on the floor if you didn't get my permission. My interest in your predicament is now fully piqued. I couldn't possibly say no!"

"You are the only one I could think of who might help me right now."

"Well, I may be Shirley Holmes, but I have none of my great-great-uncle's famous skills."

"No matter. At least you have the background. You do have a PhD."

I shook my head and replied, "But my PhD is in biochemistry and genetics. I do mathematical modeling and genetic sequencing of genetic diseases. I daresay you are more interested in doing business with a clone of Sherlock Holmes."

"You are perfect. I should introduce myself. I am Jane Mortimer, the great-grand-daughter of the one-time owner of this cane."

"Don't tell me — you are going to give me an update on the monstrous *Hound of the Baskervilles!*" My response clearly caught her off-guard.

She laughed as she replied, "If it were only so simple. No, but I must admit my concern is not about a single huge hound, but an entire bushel of hounds, for I am not a student of human skulls, but a doctor of veterinary medicine."

"Hounds — plural?"

Jane explained, "Yes — but a Baskerville hasn't died of fright. Instead, a dozen prized hounds have died for no good reason that I can discern. The breeder had me do their autopsies. He was convinced that they had been poisoned, but I could find nothing."

"No cause of death?"

"They died from lack of oxygen — but from no specific cause. That's when I thought I needed to see if they had some genetic predisposition to die young — and together."

Now I was confused. "So, what do you think?"

"No evidence of a heart or other condition. I think I need help. I found a list of experts in genetics here in America, on the other side of the pond, and saw your name."

"But I could have had no connection to Sherlock."

"I must admit that I checked you out on one of the ancestry websites and found out you ARE his distant relative, so I determined that it was fate that was bringing us together. Here I am."

"How on earth did you find me? I've even turned off email and am not using my phone! I am just renting this cottage in Ogunquit up here in Maine to get away from the university scene in Boston. I thought it might make me more 'creative' since I need to publish a research paper soon. That's the story of researchers in their early 30s — publish or perish."

"I tracked you down through your job. I knew where you worked, so I went to your university office. You weren't there, so I tried to get your department admin to tell me where you were, and she refused. So I entered the building by the back door, feeling like a real Sherlock Holmes. I found one of your grad students working in a nearby lab. She knew where you were, but also initially refused to tell me. "

"Good! I told my students to only come here in a real emergency or I would drop their grade a full grade."

Laughing, Jane continued. "But then I remembered a theater class I took as a teenager, broke into fake tears and told her you were my cousin, and our grandmother was in the hospital, so I needed to find you. She gave in, thinking that this would qualify as an emergency!"

"Jane, you are a better sleuth than I am! So — you have no ideas about the dogs?"

"I am trying not to draw premature conclusions. But this whole puppy thing just seems a bit off. I decided to clear my mind by leaving home and taking this trip to America."

"Do you have the ability to provide me with blood samples from the hounds?"

"But of course. They are in a small cool box in the boot of my car."

I found myself smiling as I replied, "What are we waiting for?" It now seemed like I might not be useless. I flung open my front door, and we stepped onto my front porch. It was at that moment that an explosion occurred at the curbside across the street.

As the smoke cleared, Jane looked on in astonishment. "That's the rear of my car that just blew up! I could have been in it! What the bloody HELL?"

"Seems to be bloody in more ways than one. Did you notice anyone following you?"

Jane shook her head. "That would be a tad more difficult than you seem to realize. I flew here from London yesterday. I currently live in far southern Cornwall near the former tin mine of Botallack. That car was a rental."

I grabbed my phone. "I'll try to take as many photos of this as I can before the police arrive!"

I immediately realized what needed to happen next and collected the appropriate supplies. "Take this plastic bag and gloves and grab anything with significant blood that you can get your hands on — and REALLY try not to cut yourself on the vials and wreckage! Then meet me back inside my cottage!"

A few minutes later, we were both back inside looking on as a trio of police cars arrived to assess the damage.

Jane collapsed in a chair and asked, "Why did you decide not to take photos and instead video the neighborhood, not just my car?"

"As you can see, the police are doing an excellent job of that! But I remember seeing a crime show where they said that arsonists love to stick around and watch the fire they started. I just had a hunch that if I videoed the scene, I might catch the bomber."

"AHH! What now?"

"Let's join the police. After all, you don't want to be blamed for the damage to the rental. Thanks for collecting the samples. If they found my fingerprints on the car, I might become their principal suspect!"

Jane and I walked to her car, acting properly shocked as if we had just noticed that the bombed car had been Jane's rental, and talked to the cops. They had plenty for their report — all of which seemed useless for us. But they did mention that it looked like a homemade overgrown incendiary device best suited for a Fourth of July beachside fireworks display. We returned inside to discuss our next steps.

I explained my plan. "Let's start by looking at the video I took. We'll hook this baby up to the TV by Bluetooth for better viewing."

"What are we looking for?"

"THAT part is easy. There's the culprit, wearing an unmarked dark baseball cap that is effectively covering his hair. See? He has turned away from my camera. He's likely a man, based on his height. Somehow, he must have known you were carrying the samples in the trunk, since he placed his home-made bomb under that area."

Jane paused before replying, "Anything to get us his name?"

"That's all we can tell unless we pick him out later because he is wearing the same cap and shirt — a highly improbable event!"

"Roll back that part. He does have a very unusual walk."

"Probably just nervous. Yet there is something — no — never mind. Just imagining."

Jane sighed as she continued, "A big dead end. Sorry to have wasted your time."

I had to smile at her lack of optimism. "Not so fast. Where is the bag you brought in?"

"Here — next to your couch."

I attempted to tease her by asking, "And you managed not to cut yourself? Didn't even cry or spit into the bag?"

Instead, Jane sounded puzzled as she replied, "Noooo."

I laughed so she might get my joke. "Then I am definitely not lost — just saves me the trouble of running worthless samples. Since all the dogs were siblings, I have what I need."

"What a relief! Mr. Peters, the breeder, insisted that I have the dogs cremated after I had done their autopsies, so I have nothing else to give you!"

"No problem. I really do have everything I need. Is it typical for owners to ask for cremation?"

"Usually I suggest that it is unnecessary, particularly for small puppies."

"But we have their blood. Just a bit weird. Does the owner know you took it?"

"I told my aunt I was taking a trip to Boston to visit a friend and for a change of scenery so she wouldn't wonder where I was. But I didn't admit to her, the breeder or anyone else that I was bringing the puppies' blood samples here. Strange that you should ask — and stranger still that someone followed me here."

I prodded her some more. This just didn't make sense. "Are you certain you did nothing else? And your aunt didn't talk to anyone?"

"I must admit that my aunt is a talker and could have said that I was flying to Boston to just about anyone. I also bought the special cool box on my way to the airport so it would fit in my suitcase. If the breeder were watching, that would have looked suspicious, I suppose."

"No one had to follow you — they just had to find out the flight you were on, and then the car you were renting. The bomber could be just a random small-time criminal for hire who was already in the U.S. It's time for you to catch a taxi and get to your hotel, relax and get some rest. We can talk again in the morning."

"I'm embarrassed to admit it, but I failed to book a room — and at the airport I was told that due to the Fourth of July festival, all the rooms in town are booked."

This was one of those times I was glad I had space for a guest. I chuckled as I said, "This couch makes into a bed. But I suspect that your clothes are gone with the car they just towed to the police lot."

"You are exactly right."

I rummaged in my dresser. "Let me grab something for you to sleep in. My supplies are low since I only signed up to stay here for a month, but I'll find something."

"Anything is fine. Remember — I showed up here unannounced!"

I was getting a bit desperate as I noted, "Anything I find is bound to be a bit loose on you — and likely way too short! Ahh! Here you go! I need to spend some time thinking. You're free to take a walk. The bomber has no interest in you, just what you had with you in that car. I'll see you in the morning. Oh — and there is a spare toothbrush in the bathroom that I haven't used!"

I decided to do some research on genetic diseases of "hounds" only to find out that the American Kennel Club — admittedly not the British equivalent — lists a total of 32 different "hound" breeds. Figuring that there might be a small smidgen of timeliness to this research, I immediately accosted Jane when she returned from her walk and wandered into the kitchen. "I'm curious as to whether you have any clue as to WHICH breed of 'hound' these puppies were."

Her reply surprised me. "Even though I'm a vet, I'm more of a cat person. Sorry. I didn't think to ask the breeder that question."

"Using Google, it was easy to find images of the various breeds as adults, but a garbled mess when I looked for puppy pictures to jog your memory!"

"Even though they were prized hounds, I found them unremarkable, except that I remember there was one runt in the litter." Jane walked to my fridge and began rummaging. "Looks like you are a bit low on food. I can walk to a store and buy some groceries."

"Most of the time I don't bother with breakfast — and then grab some takeout later in the day."

Jane laughed, but then got more serious. "You seem self-conscious about your weight. I can help you out there."

"You are certainly right that my weight needs help!"

The doctor in Jane suddenly erupted as she replied, "Most takeout is full of extra salt, fat and sugar, and because you are extra hungry having skipped breakfast, you overeat at lunch and dinner. I can be your weight-loss mentor as a way of paying you back!"

"Great idea! I need to head to my genetics lab in Boston to run some tests and will be back in a few days. Make yourself at home. You should be perfectly safe. He knows he destroyed the car's trunk — and he was so busy avoiding my photography that he wouldn't have seen you collecting the samples."

A few days later, I returned to the cottage and found Jane sitting on the couch. "I spent a very busy week at my lab — running and re-running tests to confirm what I was learning before heading back here. But as Sherlock Holmes said, 'When you have eliminated the *impossible*, whatever remains, however *improbable*, must be the truth.' Any excitement at your end?"

Jane looked much more relaxed as she replied, "No — nothing. But I have loved the sun and have had several trips to the small rocky beach. Even tried my hand at painting Edward Hopper scenes. This area is beautiful!"

"Well — I have some interesting news for you. You probably ought to sit down. You say there were 12 pups?"

Jane followed my advice and sat down. "Yes ... so?"

"I checked and the puppy deaths made the local newspaper in the Botallack area. The breeder was sad, but not financially ruined because he had insurance on them."

"He said that they were worth about 10,000 pounds each!" Jane replied.

"That's why my initial DNA test results were so interesting. It appears that all but maybe one of the dozen or so pups were half pure-bred Scottish deerhounds — and half mutt mixed with Great Dane. But something was puzzling. One of the puppies was pure-bred Scottish deerhound."

Jane leapt up, quite excited. "I know what happened! The breeder saw the pups — realized that his prized deerhound had been messing around before her fancy date when she later conceived the smaller runt — and developed a scheme to smother the pups and claim the insurance."

"He murdered them? What a fiend! Your autopsy was only for show?"

"Exactly!"

"An interesting case. This breeder Mr. Peters is an inhumane and greedy monster. I believe I have the topic of the research paper that I need to write this summer."

Jane turned away. I could tell she was sad at the prospect of leaving. "Sounds like I'm done here."

"Not so fast! You are my co-author! It will be a unique paper in all sorts of ways!"

She immediately cheered up. "I can paint some more classic Hopper landscapes — stop the insurance payout, follow the money so see who our bomber was — and ..."

"I can help on that last one. Let me give my cousin Sylvester Holmes who works for Scotland Yard a call and have him check out the money trail."

After giving Sylvester a quick call and a summary of the issue, he assured me he'd get back to me by tomorrow.

The next day, I woke up to a call from my cousin. His news meant I had to head to the living room to talk with Jane. "You probably ought to sit down again. We have a smidge of a problem. There is no money trail — and no evidence of any unordinary cash withdrawals. The bomber was not paid — at least not paid by Mr. Peters. And because there is no money trail showing he conspired with the bomber, we can't stop the insurance payout. Our bomber and Mr. Peters may get away with this!"

Jane became excited. "Call me crazy, but I have another idea. On this case, everyone seems to be related to someone else. What if the bomber was related to the breeder — and thus trusted him to pay him after the insurance payout?"

That really was a great idea. It even surprised me. "Let me call Sylvester again and see the names of the people whose phones were near our front door that morning — and see if by any chance one has the same last name as the breeder!"

I paced as I made the call. Since he didn't answer, I was forced to leave a voicemail message summarizing Jane's idea. It was not until the next morning when my cell rang that I could talk with him. "A phone in our area is owned by a Jonathan

Randolph Peters of BOSTON? He's a student there? BLOODY HELL! I know that scumbag. That's why I vaguely recognized his walk! He's one of my genetics students — always asking questions about dogs instead of people. He's a know-it-all chemistry grad student who needed some waivers to get into my class. But I know him as J.R. — J.R. Peters. No wonder he had such an easy time tracking us down! I told all of my grad students where I was staying. You say he's the nephew of the breeder? That proves insurance fraud! Get on with it! Lock them both up! While I'm at it, I'll flunk him in the seminar I'm teaching."

Jane was grinning as I hung up since she had overheard us. "He must have followed me from the airport to your house and lab in Boston, recognized your home and lab, and realized that I was trying to see YOU — and thus I wanted to get genetic testing done on the dogs remains."

"Thus, when he found us together here, he used a homemade Fourth of July device to damage your car and destroy the evidence you had carried here!" I replied.

"Shirley, you and I did it — proving once again that blood is thicker than water in these cases. AND I guarantee you'll lose 20 pounds this summer with my cooking and coaching!"

"I am as addicted to sugar and fat and salt as Sherlock was to opium. So if you succeed, I'll visit you and vacation in Cornwall next summer to lose another 20 pounds!"

Mila Getmansky Sherman

Sense Symphony

By Mila Getmansky Sherman

<u>I woke up to hear</u> an owl hooting outside of my window. I opened the shades and saw an owl perched on a large branch of our magnificent oak tree. The owl was visible as it was bathing in the moonlight, today being a full blood moon. The owl's presence was majestic, almost magical. I couldn't believe what I saw, it was too surreal, so I closed my eyes.

<u>I opened</u> my eyes and now I saw two chipmunks sitting on the branch where before the owl was sitting. I blinked and blinked, hoping to see the owl and only half believing that chipmunks could climb such a magnificent tree and precariously position themselves on the branch which was now swinging with the wind. What were the chipmunks thinking?

<u>I could smell</u> the moisture in the air, with rain slowly dripping through the leaves of the magnificent oak. I could also smell the fear of the chipmunks who stupidly decided to go on a midnight adventure and found themselves holding onto their lives by a thread, being exposed to the wind and all nature's elements. I could smell the freshness of the night, a comfortable

breeze, not only touching me gently, but penetrating my skin's pores and making me actually smell the breeze. I leaned over to have that smell penetrate all my body, even raising my toes to feel the whole power and awesomeness of the breeze.

I could almost taste the breeze. I understood subconsciously that it was vapor, H_2O molecules to be exact. But I still stuck out my tongue hoping to taste the divine nectar. This nectar will transform me to a different state of mind, more blissful, where things might not make sense, but I will not care. Where all senses interconnect to make a unique symphony that is never to be repeated again. Those senses are rather balanced in contrast to a cacophony of competing smells/tastes/senses.

I touch my lips, my forehead, my hair, my shoulders, I move my hand around, there is a bedstand, the bed, softness of sheets. I have not really moved away from my bed, I was not hallucinating or dreaming, I was a recipient and active participant of the sense symphony. I took a large breath, took it all in and went back to sleep.

Hedgehog in the Fog

By Mila Getmansky Sherman

I like this secret walking
in the fog;
— Charles Reznikoff, *Autobiography Hollywood*

There is something amazing about the fog. It is the least predictable meteorological phenomenon. You often do not expect it. When you wake up, you think whether the day is going to be sunny, cloudy or rainy. Will there be torrential rain for your outdoor party? Will it be a hot humid day making you sleepy throughout the afternoon? Will the rain stop you from your daily run? The fog is shrouded in mystery. On a given day, it just rolls in quickly, dimming the slightest flicker of the sunlight and creating a thick and impenetrable layer of a humid, almost humanoid form. The fog makes you wonder. You do not know when it began and definitely have no idea when it will end. There are no boundaries to it and no sharp edges. Our brain works hard to identify its forms — a cloud, a person, a steeple, a house, a gigantic magic carpet. As soon as one shape is formed, it is transformed, dynamically changing right in front of your eyes. You just keep still, cannot plan, cannot think, only feel, sense and be in awe.

I vividly remember "Hedgehog in the Fog," a Russian animated film that to me always felt like an infinity. The hedgehog gets lost in the fog — there is no beginning or end to it, he cannot plan, so he just succumbs to being there. In the beginning the hedgehog is overcome with fear, and he starts seeing things and shapes — a falling leaf can be a monster and something for sure is hiding in a hollow of a tree trunk. He is overcome with fear, starts fidgeting, running, and then falls into a river. He is surrounded by fog and water with no idea of where he is going. At some point he lets go. The hedgehog says to itself: "I am the river, let the river carry me along." He sighs deeply and begins to float in with the current.

For predicting the fog, there is no equivalent to the "My Radar" app to tell you when the storm will pass, or meteorologists telling you when the heat wave will subside. The study of fog predictability is at its infancy with researchers and governments trying to capture, measure and predict this elusive phenomenon. In some places like San Francisco and Mendocino, the fog is a constant presence due to extreme temperature differentials between coastal and inland California.

However, in most places in the world, the fog is often a big unknown. Once in a while, in our predictable and planned lives, the fog drapes us like a blanket. Time freezes, and we just go with the flow — all senses that serve us well in our daily lives, like smell, direction, touch, are useless. No need to be agitated, just go with the flow, and breathe into the expansive surroundings.

I remember as a child thinking what is the point of that "Hedgehog in the Fog" film? Which lesson are we learning? That hedgehog has no sense of direction, does not know how to use GPS or the phone, and seems lost. He is certainly not an example of a striver or goal setter. He decides to be one with the mystery of the fog, he does not wait for the fog to pass, and the sun to appear. He is one with his new medium.

This hedgehog definitely does not have an A-type personality, he is not a leader, is not hiking or exercising, and is not socializing with friends. However, his mere still presence, his mindfulness of the wonder happening around him, makes me feel that we often do not notice such precious moments in our rushed, timed and goal-oriented lives. It is important to stop, feel, be at one with the surroundings, and surrender.

Alternative Lives

By Mila Getmansky Sherman

Here comes a famous ski jumper. She is fearless, she stands up at the top of the ski jump, looking into the abyss. Below is a smooth convex surface of the ski jump ramp. She is steady, practically steely. She looks far into the horizon, testing — almost tasting — the wind. She is sleek and determined. And then she jumps, increasing her speed right before she leaps into the air. She is parallel with her skis, she has great form and she soars like a bird. She is now one with the wind, traveling at the speed of a bullet. This whole experience happened in a blink of an eye, but for her it was a lifetime.

Step Up: How Risk-Taking and Networks Create Opportunities for Women

By Mila Getmansky Sherman

This past summer, I took my daughter Daniella to the Smithsonian Museum of Natural History in Washington, D.C. When we arrived, it was announced that the tarantula would be having its daily meal. As we came to the feeding area there were lots of kids surrounding the glass box with the tarantula inside. The docent started talking about tarantulas, their habitat, what they eat, that despite the ominous way they look, there have never been any recorded human casualties due to tarantula bites, and so on. Then she announced that she was about to feed the tarantula, but since it was daytime and they're fed at night, they're very sensitive to light and especially to sudden movements. So, she said, please, take two steps back and do not move. What happened next was amazing. Imagine the social experiment that was unraveling right before my eyes. The previously homogeneous group of curious kids seemingly split, with girls diligently taking two steps back and not moving, and boys rushing to the center of exhibit, with several actually peering in through the now-open glass cage. The docent had to wave them back before feeding the tarantula. My daughter and I looked at each other and she also noted this gender-based risk behavior. Some of this risk taking is biologically innate. I'm not trying to rewire you ladies to disobey instructions and have you touch the scary-looking spider. But what my daughter and I noticed is, there was a reward for those who rushed in. The boys got to see the spider up close, eating and moving, and the girls only saw something furry, at a distance, behind the glass that was now all fogged up. Were the boys crazy for not listening to all the instructions? Remember, the docent did say that nobody has ever died from tarantula bites. So that risk clearly paid off for those who took it.

Risk and reward are intimately linked. As a finance professor at the University of Massachusetts Amherst, I introduce the concept of risk to our finance students in their first class. You cannot talk about financial opportunities or rewards without explicitly discussing risks. To navigate opportunities, you need to take more risks. Risk and opportunity are two sides of the same coin. In finance we teach that to assess the risk of, say, your investment portfolio, you need to identify the source of risk and measure your exposure to that risk. Likewise, to navigate opportunities, you need to both identify opportunities and show up to claim them. Men are typically more risk-taking than women in their personal and professional lives. So, it is important for women to increase our risk tolerance and learn how to navigate opportunities.

In finance, where risk-taking behavior is generously rewarded, fewer than 20 percent of positions are occupied by women. Sadly, women are missing out. Even in academic finance, my colleague Heather Tookes and I found that only

15 percent of finance professors are women. As students choose their majors and get advice while going through college, they are lacking female role models and mentors who can help them to jump-start their careers.

Decisions such as managing personal finances, understanding financial markets and being able to navigate financial crises should not be the sole domain of men. This is not just a personal wish, but actually it is a rational conclusion. In addition to being taught about risk and return, all our students are taught that to decrease the risk of their assets they have to diversify across different investments. You do not make smart investments by buying stocks concentrating on one industry, such as technology, manufacturing or banking. You do not put all your eggs in one basket.

Diversification simply makes sense. It means adding different voices at the decision-making table and having different approaches to assessing risk. Men tend to be more overconfident, and according to research, overconfidence leads to lower investment returns. So, having women on the investment team adds to the bottom line because women bring different opinions, ways of investing and ways of calculating risk. A recent McKinsey report showed that companies in the top quartile for gender diversity are more likely to have greater financial returns compared to their peers. So, if you are an individual, a company or a pension fund, see who manages your money. Are there women on the investment team? If the answer is yes, they will make you more money.

Women: In order to succeed, you do not need to become men. You can come as you are — but you do need to show up. You will need to take that risk.

Next time you are interviewing for a job in a male-dominated field, use this argument that women add value. It does not have to be finance. Research shows that women represent only 26 percent of the workforce in all science, technology, engineering and math (STEM) fields.

So, how do you navigate opportunities? One way is to push forward, literally. Recently our UMASS Women in Finance was one of the two student groups invited to be on the New York Stock Exchange floor when the opening bell rang. Ringing the bell is a huge deal. Everybody at the stock exchange is looking at you, not to mention that the whole event is broadcast internationally. It is a one-in-a-lifetime opportunity and an amazing honor to be invited. Another student group from a different university (happened to be all men) stood all front and center, blocking all of our women. Colleen Collins, our student leader, used her elbows to get not just herself but the whole group of women to share the center stage. They clearly showed up and grabbed that once-in-a-lifetime opportunity. Colleen later told me that other women told her not to make a fuss and just stay behind. Ladies, as Colleen clearly demonstrated, you have to not only show up, but make a fuss. And remember, she did not use elbows to just elevate herself, but brought all the other women with her.

Now, not all of us have as much gumption as Colleen to navigate opportunities, so a more subtle approach is suggested. While in graduate school, thanks to my mentor Andrew Lo, I had an opportunity to get an internship at a bank on Wall Street. I was so excited, as a student of finance, to learn how banks work and how financial trades are made, and personally learn from seasoned traders. In my first week I was asked to make photocopies, and lots of them. Full disclosure, I did not have much experience with copy machines and I'm generally not good with mechanical tools. Within the first hour, I jammed the whole copy machine and a technician had to be called in. Trying to keep me away from something I could break or spill, my bosses assigned me to sit with a trader for the rest of my internship and learn from him all the nuts and bolts of finance, trading and financial markets.

This is what I had wanted and it definitely helped me with my future career in finance. Just imagine if I'd done a perfect job of making copies, collating them, even color coding and sorting them, oh my. I'm not saying that you should jam copiers to get ahead. But a happy accident can be an opportunity. Make sure to grab those opportunities and do not go back to perfect the art of photocopying. What I am saying is take happy accidents and calculated risks and convert them into opportunities. These lead to the rewards that men are already ahead of us in reaping.

While you may be a risk-taker, I am not. No matter how many reasons my friend Jeanne Hardy gives me to go downhill skiing with her, I always find an excuse to say no. Jeanne says: It will feel great (me: I do not like speed). Jeanne says: We will all have fun skiing with our families and friends (me: I would rather be doing taxes in the skiing lodge). I give her more excuses: (me: I do not see anything), (she: get contact lenses), (me: I do not know how to put them on), (Jeanne: I will do it for you). She is very convincing, but I am not going to be swayed to ski down that mountain.

So, for those of us who are risk averse, here is the secret sauce that men have been using to navigate opportunities (be it on the golf course or the boardroom): The power of social networks. I am not talking about social media, but true and meaningful connections between people. As a part of the social network, you do not have to re-engineer yourself and become a risk taker. You just need to know people like Jeanne who are.

We are all social creatures. Even though there are 7.7 billion people on our Mother Earth, we are all remarkably interconnected. For example, Julia, who is sitting right here, and I have one degree of separation. A school teacher in Ghana whom I have never met and I have six degrees of separation. The closer the community, the smaller the number of degrees. For example, in our Easthampton and Amherst communities we are probably separated by only two degrees. How many times do you go to an event and meet people you know or meet somebody with whom you share a common acquaintance? We love our circle of friends and confidantes.

Michelle Obama in her memoir "Becoming" eloquently and passionately described the power of her social circle that has sustained her through years in Chicago, Washington, D.C., and beyond. Women in Michelle's circle were there for each other to help with babysitting, provide unbiased opinions, and support each other during hard personal and professional times. We all could benefit from Michelle's wisdom of forming such nourishing circles. Such circles are based on trust. I propose to build on these trust-based circles and go a step further. Form networks that are sustainable, strong, far-reaching, that empower everybody in the network, focus on network diversity, and have a way of identifying people outside of the network who will benefit greatly by being a part of it.

The power of social networks, or how people are interconnected, has been studied in multiple disciplines such as social sciences, sociology, political science and beyond. I will concentrate on how it works in finance.

In finance, even if your primary bank is the local savings bank, and you have no risky investments, you were negatively affected in the recent financial crisis of 2008–09. Why? Because financial institutions are interrelated. The risk of the financial system, or as we call it in the financial world, systemic risk, is measured as the interconnectedness between different types of financial institutions such as banks, brokerage firms, insurance companies, hedge funds and even sovereigns (foreign countries). Despite what we've been told, the financial crisis of 2008–09 cannot be blamed on one bank failure or one group of people who couldn't afford to pay their mortgages. The systemic risk had been gradually increasing and peaked before the crisis. Not understanding the power of such increasing connections cost the economy and population greatly. When the economy is booming, close connections lead to faster and more efficient ways of executing financial transactions, transferring money, lending and spreading the risk. However, when things are bad, such connections can lead to the cascade of losses from one financial institution to another.

It is important to understand the networks of financial institutions to explain and hopefully prevent financial crises. Social networks are very much like financial networks. We can use the same principles of understanding the power of interconnectedness to navigate opportunities. Social networks not only nourish you but provide you with lasting social connections, open doors for you and give you a wonderful opportunity to lift others. It is a virtuous cycle that keeps on giving. Last year I had an opportunity to create such a network when Colleen Collins (remember that brave lady who made the fuss on the NYSE floor?) was the only woman in my financial modeling honors class. She and I looked at each other and decided to do something to increase the number of women students in finance. We started a Women in Finance Club which grew from one person last year to 70 members this year. The young women are now a part of the nationally recognized Smart Women Securities started at Harvard, which educates young women about finance and investments and opens networking opportunities by introducing them to successful finance professionals. Women network with each other and help each other work on resumes and find job opportunities. Our women students are also there for fellow group members — to bounce ideas off one another and empower each other to take risks and identify great opportunities.

It is important to understand the structure of social networks. In the academic literature, social networks are a function of nodes (in this case people) and edges (in this case connections). In order for you to be a part of the network, you need to form a connection. However, not all nodes and connections are the same. Some nodes are central (like people who run the group or connect to most people in the group), or peripheral (people who might only have a few other connections). Think about a body as a network of organs. The heart and brain are central nodes while toes are peripheral.

While both women and men benefit from networking opportunities, they tend to network differently. A recent Harvard Business School study found that both men and women MBAs who landed executive leadership positions benefited from being central in the MBA student networks, meaning they were connected to multiple hubs, or people who have lots of contacts across different groups of students. However, for women, being central in the social network was not enough, they had to also have a strong inner circle of close female contacts. In my research with Heather Tookes we find that in order to get tenure in a finance discipline in business schools, publication in journals is the most important factor. Women and men tend to have a similar number of solo-authored papers in top journals; however, women tend to have fewer co-authored publications. When they do co-author, they tend to co-author more with other women. The implication is that women are not networked enough. Women need to meet central nodes of the academic network, and these nodes are mostly men. Women can greatly benefit from networks that will introduce them to more people (and not just women) with whom they can co-author research papers, thus opening more opportunities for women in finance.

So, how do we navigate opportunities? First, we need to identify opportunities that will truly benefit us and then we must show up. Next, we must increase our risk tolerance. One of the best ways to do this is by growing and then tapping your social network to propel yourself forward. Take the risk, show up and introduce yourself. You can start it right now, right here, and meet all other bold and brilliant women on and off stage. Introduce yourself. Create opportunities for yourself and others. But please, remember to look around, identify those who are not in the network, who can be helped by being a part of it — invite them, and lift them up so all can benefit. That is the power of social networks.

Adapted From:

TEDxEasthamptonWomen
Originally Presented December 2019
Revised

https://www.ted.com/talks/
mila_getmansky_sherman_step_up_how_risk_taking_network
s_create_opportunities_for_women

D'var Torah for My Adult Bat Mitzvah

By Mila Getmansky Sherman

In this week's Torah portion God commands: "There shall be no needy among you." Torah gives us lots of examples of how to ensure that there is not a permanent underclass in our society. If people have hardships, there are provisions that every third year everybody should bring out a full tithe (one tenth) of their yield and leave it to orphans, widows and Levites. Such charity is required of all in the community and helps the poor and people with no land to subsist on. Torah also understands the negative implications of debt. And prevents personal bankruptcies by requiring that every seventh year everybody shall practice the remission of debt. This helps for the society to flourish and prevents a downward spiral into poverty.

The Torah specifically provides for people's self-reliance and independence. A servant has to be freed on the seventh year. In addition, the Torah specifically aims to prevent people from starting penniless and thereby increasing the probability of being indebted and becoming servants again. When freeing servants, they shall be given capital and supplies in order for them to live an independent life and minimize chances of becoming indebted again.

Even in tranquil economic times, there is poverty and injustice on local and global levels. During these especially trying months of hardship, compounded by the fact that soup kitchens, religious buildings and shelters are closed, what can we do? How can we fulfill this mitzvah that "there should be no needy among you" while respecting social distancing rules?

I believe we are invited now to be creative and heartful to avoid even more socioeconomic disparity. Yes, life might seem chaotic, we are overwhelmed, so it might be tempting to protect yourself and your immediate family circle first and postpone thinking about the needy.

Maimonides mentions that the highest level of charity is enabling somebody to be self-supporting. Individually and as a part of the community we are finding innovative ways of raising money for local businesses — online ordering from local farms, continuing to pay those who do gardening and housecleaning even if we do not use their services during these times, for example.

How can you enable somebody to be self-supporting? Which skill can you teach those in need? Some of us who are finance professionals and educators are teaching financial literacy skills. Think about all the schoolchildren whose school is canceled and for whom all summer camps and activities are canceled. Can you share a skill with such kids to empower both them and their parents? I encourage us all to think of ways we can support each other and fulfill the mitzvah, especially in these trying times.

We are reminded every morning — in the first blessing of the morning — to remove sleep from our eyes and slumber from our eyelids:

בָּרוּךְ אַתָּה יהוה אֱלֹהֵינוּ חַי הָעוֹלָמִים
הַמַּעֲבִיר שֵׁנָה מֵעֵינַי וּתְנוּמָה מֵעַפְעַפָּי׳

Baruch atah adonay, eloheynu melech ha'olam, hama'avir shenah me'eynay utnumah me'afapay.

Blessed are You, source of all, who removes sleep from my eyes and slumber from my eyelids.

In these times let us take it to mean moving beyond our usual understanding of what we are capable of and opening our eyes and hearts to see deeply what we can offer to others.

Judith Silverstein

Toast on Your 40th

By Judith Silverstein

I lift a glass
To let you know
By inspiring example
That you can still
That it's not too late
To lose your job, your purpose, and your direction
Or to have never yet found them
To be devastated by sex
To have untapped potential
To make a fool of yourself
To act like a child
To get a trashy tattoo just above your behind
For eventual home-care attendants to find

And to feel all of it more deeply than ever before
With greater clarity and resonance
Than you ever wished possible

Prospects improve
For rendering public service
As a negative example to others

There is still time
To develop irritating refrains
To discover new regrets
To be out of excuses
To be referred to as a big boy or girl
Who knows better
And still do whatever it is anyway
Making up for lost confidence with increased tenacity

For the first time, some things will no longer be possible
Though they might not be the things you think
But you won't know that until even later
Because this is probably not the end
Even if you sometimes might not mind if it were
In that interim stage, when enthusiasm flags
Just before you begin to grasp
That the end is real, and will pull in shortly
The most crowded commuter train of all time
So what the hell's the rush

There will, however, be increased opportunities
For taking out your frustrations on others
And for letting them down
As well as for investing in efforts benefiting humanity
Or at least some person
That won't be appreciated until much later
Like after you're dead
Or, say, never

Patterns begin to confirm themselves
And this is terribly, terribly interesting
Even as insights arrive shortly after their use-by date
And no one else can use them, either

Your mistakes are less forgivable
Your quirks less charming
But don't worry — there will be more of them
And you may be lucky enough to have someone near
Who is meanwhile becoming increasingly blind to them
Maybe even someone besides yourself
As your vanity steadily increases
In inverse proportion to its justification

Your body will require more respect and cultivation
And will betray you anyway
You expect that, but what you don't expect
Is that it may be more beautiful than ever
Like the rest of this shit
That was already happening anyway
Whether you knew it or not
As your defenses fall away
And the world is revealed

Commencement: A 10-Minute Play

By Judith Silverstein

Cast of Characters

Dean Fairfax	A distinguished man in his early 60s, in academic regalia
Daphne Fleischman	A white woman in her 50s, in a floral summer dress
Dreadlocks Grad	Graduating student, cap and gown, hair in dreadlocks
White Female Grad	Graduating student, female, 21; white, pretty, voice heavy on the California upspeak and vocal fry

Frat Guy Grad	Graduating student, 21, wearing red baseball cap
Handsome Grad	Graduating student, handsome male with longish hair, Byronic type, 21
Father of White Female Grad	An imposing white man in his 50s, in expensive suit and tie
4 Interchangeable Grads (Crowd) Grad #1, Grad #2, Grad #3, Grad #4	Four graduating students in cap and gown

Setting

Graduation ceremony at Stanford University. A perfect June afternoon under a halcyon blue sky. There is a sunlit stage where the speaker's podium is placed and dignitaries are assembled; a white canopy billows above the seated crowd.

DEAN FAIRFAX
Ladies and gentlemen, welcome to the Achievement Keynote for the 125th Commencement at Stanford University, where each year we invite distinguished guests to reflect on the nature of achievement.

Our first speaker is someone you never heard of, and with good reason. Born into privilege and showing promise in her youth, by the time she reached middle age she had used her considerable opportunities to achieve practically nothing. By the age of 50, she was unemployed and collecting government benefits. She has an unfinished PhD, a cluster of autoimmune diseases, and no discernible career. By now you surely have no idea whom I'm speaking of — please welcome Daphne Fleischman.

(Crowd murmurs. Scattered applause.)

DAPHNE
Thank you. Good afternoon, graduates, parents, families, administrators and faculty. Congratulations graduating class!

(Pause. Muffled whoops and applause from crowd.)

Ladies and gentlemen. People often ask me: given the opportunities and privileges that you've had, how is it that you've achieved the level of failure that you have without recourse to drugs or alcohol, insanity or trauma?

I'm here today to answer that question. To talk to you about failure — what it is and what it isn't, and how you can achieve it.

I didn't really prepare, so I'm just going to open up the floor for questions. But before I do, I want to dispel a pervasive and troubling misconception. In Silicon Valley you hear a lot of

217

talk these days to the effect that there is no such thing as failure, only opportunities to learn.

(Shudders.)

Ugh, *learning*. Ladies and gentlemen, the idea is to *not* learn. Or better yet, to learn too late. That's what we're talking about today — the irredeemable, the irreparable, the unutterable, the pointless. So if you could confine your questions to that realm without holding failure hostage to success, I would really appreciate it.

(Points to audience.)

Yes, you in the front row. Please stand up.

GRADUATE #1
(Confused.)

Um, *who* exactly are you?

DAPHNE
Let me fill in a few details. After graduating from a top university I turned down a job in a law firm in favor of night work as a photographer's assistant. I kicked around for a while in a dead-end relationship with my college boyfriend before heading off to California to flame out in a PhD program in the humanities here at Stanford, where I never finished my dissertation.

GRADUATE #1
(More wondering than hostile.)

And they would invite you here *why*?

DAPHNE
I'm not exactly sure. Maybe they were thinking that by now I'd have an inspiring story of learning and resilience. Oops. But I am an expert of sorts, so maybe it's a case of the mysterious ecumenical wisdom of academe.

GRADUATE #1
Uh, thanks …

(Sits.)

DAPHNE
You there, in the second row.

GRADUATE #2
Did you have any early indications that this would be your path? Like in childhood?

DAPHNE
By the age of five I was already exhibiting the kind of convoluted reasoning that became my hallmark. But that could have been harnessed in any direction. It's like music. Some people have a gift, but you have to learn to use it. I had some harsh words earlier for learning, but not all learning is constructive. It's actually hugely important in failure.

219

GRADUATE #2

Won't our top-notch education and high intelligence prevent that kind of learning?

DAPHNE

Studies show that the most significant failures require intelligence and training, often a good deal of it. That's where a university education can come into play — cultivating your bad habits, sequestering you from experience, informing you about things to worry about, introducing you to insidious ideologies. Your education has given you access to the crippling nonsense not just of your own time, but of the ages. Don't be afraid to use it.

(Points.)

Yes?

GRADUATE #3
(Stands.)

Can you comment on the influence of family? What do you do if there's no big trauma or strong negative examples there?

(Sits.)

DAPHNE

If possible develop a fake personality you use to please your parents and teachers. Or find a mentor outside your usual circle of family and friends. Reach out.

It's a myth that failure necessarily involves isolation. It can be accomplished alone, yes, and often is. But sometimes it takes two to fail. Whole families excel at it — whole communities, nations, the human race. It takes a village to fail a child, as a magnificently failed presidential candidate once said. Women, I think, have an edge here. Who more than us knows that failure is nothing if you can't share it with someone, and pass it on?

GRADUATE #3
It sounds like you're saying failure is social and historical. What about individual responsibility?

DAPHNE
Many people confuse failure and bad luck, including the bad luck of history. Taking advantage of disadvantage can be highly effective, but for my money squandering a good hand is really the higher form. It doesn't count if powerful overlords have done the job for you through persecution or oppression. You have to be throwing away opportunity.

DREADLOCKS GRAD
(Stands.)

It seems to me your definition is highly culture and class specific. Are you saying marginalized groups don't have access to failure? Like, Black people can't even *fail*?

DAPHNE
(With pride.)

No one ever told me I couldn't do anything, or beat me, or arrested me, or discouraged me. I had to do everything myself.

DREADLOCKS GRAD
Oh, come on! That's just defining failure so it can be monopolized by the privileged.

DAPHNE
(Authoritatively lecturing.)

You bring up a couple of important points. First, everyone is born with *some* promise to squander. Second, there's a lot of great work being done in the area of internalizing historical trauma, really making it your own. Point taken — I shouldn't dismiss that very significant field of endeavor just because it's not my specialty, though as a woman I like to think I'm not a total stranger to the field.

DREADLOCKS GRAD
Man, you really are twisted. You're claiming to be a failure, so, like, humble. But you're really kind of condescending and arrogant.

DAPHNE
(Blinking, frozen, yet masochistically thrilled.)

Yes … you're seeing how close success is to failure. The emptiness of mastery. Arrogance and devaluing others are core principles.

DREADLOCKS GRAD

Aw man, this is bullshit. You're just doing this Zen failure thing so you can't lose any more than you already have.

(Sits down, crossing his arms in disgust. Then mutters under his breath.)

That's some *poser bullshit.*

DAPHNE

(Pleased to have failed again, but also genuinely losing her composure.)

It seems I've once again succeeded in …

(Breaks off. Gazes out into the audience, shading her eyes as if against a glare, uncertain as to what to do next.)

Is there anyone else who has any questions … ?

DEAN FAIRFAX

(Hastily, to the rescue.)

I have a question, Ms. Fleischman.

(DAPHNE is gazing off into space, blinking as if tears might be imminent.)

Ms. Fleischman?

(DEAN FAIRFAX clears throat nervously, but perseveres with what he hopes is a softball question.)

In my teaching career I come across a lot of students who procrastinate. Can you comment on that?

DAPHNE
(Relieved, grateful, retrieving her grandeur.)

Ah. Thank you, Dean Fairfax. Procrastination is so vital that I was hoping to avoid dealing with it because I can't take the pressure. But since you ask, I'll just say this: Keep it simple. Get rid of your goals and there's nothing to procrastinate about. Some of my colleagues think that's a suspiciously constructive approach, and prefer hardcore, direct procrastination. I did that earlier in life, and I still do, in a way. But I hardly notice it now because I've so thoroughly lost sight of my goals.

GRADUATE #4
You mean live in the moment?

DAPHNE
No, I advise against that. True, it may lead to a promising lack of planning and foresight. But there's always the risk that it can lead to pleasure and, worse, enlightenment. You've got to be miserable, fearing the present, yes, but also regretting the past and dreading the future. It's tricky. You don't actually let go of goals, because that could be liberating. You have to maintain a sense that you should be achieving something. But

224

keep it vague. (Points into audience, half-proud to have recovered her composure.)

Yes? You in the back?

FRAT GUY GRAD
(Sarcastic.)

So why don't we all just go ahead and commit suicide?

DAPHNE
(Taking it seriously, back on her high horse.)

Get it out of your head that we're talking about the dramatic here — suicides, conflagrations. These are perhaps failures in the obvious sense of the word. Yet they display a certain sense of decisiveness, of grandeur, that betrays the cause. For what failure is truly complete without living long enough to savor it?

(Points into audience.)

Yes, you?

WHITE FEMALE GRAD
(Heavy on the California upspeak and vocal fry.)

Um, excuse me? How is this appropriate when we're celebrating our graduation from college? The beginning of the most exciting part of our lives?

225

DAPHNE

You don't just plunge downward from birth. Failure is a life arc with its own rhythms. That's why I made sure to graduate from a good school: To truly fail, you need to display promise. For what is failure without some better outcome to compare oneself to?

WHITE FEMALE GRAD'S FATHER
(Imposing himself protectively in front of his daughter in prosecutorial style.)

I think what my daughter means is, what are you trying to prove here? What's your point? Do you think you're a comedian? Is this ironic? You're not Conan O'Brien, that's for sure. Are you Andy Kaufman? Bartleby the Scrivener?

DAPHNE
(Blinking as tears begin to well again.)

I don't know what I'm doing. I never have. It wasn't my idea to come here, but I did say yes. I think I'm still trying to please the authorities —
(Puts her face in her hands.)

WHITE FEMALE GRAD'S FATHER
I see, the authorities. So this is social critique. Or is this just mainly about you? That's what it is, isn't it? Didn't finish your dissertation, getting even with those who did? A little revenge on others more successful than you, and on the system you couldn't compete in? It's the most selfish thing I've ever seen!

This isn't about the graduates, their day, their accomplishments — it's about you!

(DAPHNE, humiliated, starts to leave the stage, her hand over her face.)

HANDSOME GRAD
(Stands, raises his hand.)

Wait a minute. All that is clearly true. But aren't many successful people acting out narcissistic compulsions? Conforming to or reacting against authorities? Trying to get laid? Why should Doris What's-Her-Name here be any different?

DAPHNE
It's Daphne. Daphne, not Doris. I'm not trying to be different. Not anymore.

HANDSOME GRAD
(Carried away with his own eloquence.)

Isn't there something dehumanizing about our relentless cult of achievement that makes some very fine people who might otherwise have something to give just break down and quit, like Dolores here? Everyone knows that. Everyone pays lip service to how wrong it is. But they keep the whole thing going. By laying all that bare, isn't this embarrassing show really a sort of success, and of a reasonably conventional, constructive sort?

DAPHNE

Please don't say that. I don't want my suffering to be co-opted as a success story. I promised myself I would not allow that.

(Face in hands, crying.)

HANDSOME GRAD
(Still carried away, oblivious to Daphne.)

Who cares if the successful are just projecting their dark compulsions on the world? Isn't that what we want? Isn't that what we lash them on to do? Isn't that why it's not surprising that the results are death and destruction?

FRAT GUY GRAD
(Shouts from his seat.)

Yeah! What the world needs is more *losers*!

DAPHNE
(Ignoring FRAT GUY GRAD, addressing HANDSOME GRAD.)
Thank you, young man. A fellow romantic. In another time, another place, I would have liked to know you better.

HANDSOME GRAD
Ugh. Please don't say that.

DAPHNE
I'm sorry. I don't know who I am anymore.

228

(DAPHNE freezes. She wants to get off the stage, but she also wants to stay on it.)

WHITE FEMALE GRAD'S FATHER
(Muttering under his breath.)

I'll say you're sorry.

(Aloud, standing indignantly, waving to DEAN FAIRFAX.)

Dean Fairfax? I don't know what you were thinking here, but don't you think we've had enough of suffering humanity?

DEAN FAIRFAX
(Hurries to the podium and steps in front of Daphne.)

Thank you, Ms. Fleischman. Commencement celebrants, let's give Ms. Fleischman a round of applause. She may not agree with that assessment, nor may you. But as fallen comedy idol Woody Allen once said, 80 percent of success is showing up. Eighty percent, Ms. Fleischman. That's a B.

(A confused mixture of applause and boos from the CROWD.)

END

Linda Walls

Pot and Indy

By Linda Walls

High on a window ledge, an orange pot with blue dots gazes into the clear, dark sky. Treetops and stars span the arc of night. Wafts of air, scented in possibility, prompt in Pot the thought to rise aloft, surrounded by space and starlight, to hover, to watch and relax while counting meteorites. Swiftly, a downdraft drives Pot's thoughts earthward, to the lower ledge, further from sky and near brook, its plants, banks and bottom bed, its silt, pebbles and leaf debris in water carrying every drop, gurgle, babble and splash to somewhere, leaving Pot to ponder how far brook's somewhere may be.

The wind hastens, ground squirrels scurry, the back gate bangs, leaves scatter, lids clatter and the teakettle clangs. Pot's attention returns to the window ledge and hears owl hoots, creaking branches, shaking leaves and a persimmon drop, bringing Pot to a brink where listening ends, frustration builds and yearning begins.

"All life is outside, in the dark, in the sky, the trees, the kitchen even, everywhere but here, in me," Pot bellows from the ledge. Inside Pot, blue bumps the size of baby fists begin to push and poke Pot, who barks, "What's all this!?" No answer, more pushing and poking, pressing and pulls. Pot calls again, "Why the commotion?" Still no answer, and Pot ignores the ruckus, to think back to being clay in the ground, dug-up and gathered, formed into a large lump, and thrown on a wheel to spin between hands as warm as afternoon sunshine.

Pot remembers the robins and wrens darting between blooms above the windowsill next to the drying rack where Pot waited to dry. "Waiting was easy then, but hard now. I wanted so little, and now I want so much. Why is that? Indy, where are you?"

Awakened now, a large glazed indigo blue dot on Pot sputters in reply, "Is something wrong, Pot? What's the matter?"

"Me, I matter. I want to be free like the creatures outside, fish in the brook, wind in trees, birds above me, free. I want to fly!"

"What's gotten into you?"

"You tell me, Indy. Your dots punch and poke me inside and out. I'll be bent out of shape and break."

"The dots are your dots too, Pot, you need to know how to calm dots."

"I'm not calm, how can I calm the dots, they're not like you, they're like babies who don't know what they want."

"Do you know what you want, Pot?"

"I want to breathe new air. I want to feel the thrum of sound in space."

"What's wrong with being the beautifully bright pot you already are?"

"Wrong? I'm a pot on a ledge, too beautiful to be used."

"Being used is overrated and, instead, we dots play: checkers, tiddlywinks and solitaire if we must. We sing and whistle with the wind, the best play of all."

"Who hears you over the wind?"

"Who cares, but you would, if you listen. We dots are like leaves on trees, ripples in lakes and dewdrops at morning. We come, and we go."

"That's me, but I want to go, like you and your indigo glaze get-up-and-go I admire so, the way you go-go-go every which where. Why else would I call you Indy?"

"Because I'm indigo blue?"

"That too, but because of how you get around. You're on me, then off me, then you're off the shelf, all by yourself!"

"Being a dot is cool."

"Cool yes, and independent! Indy, why won't you help me calm the dots?"

"Are you and the dots talking yet?"

"I called out, once, twice, no answer, so I called you."

"Woke me, I was asleep, but calling a third time might be a charm. The dots want you to play, with them!"

"Play! My interest now is in the sky and the brook."

"The dots don't know that, they push and pull you instead."

"I want it to stop."

"Then do something about it."

"I don't *know* what to do. I know you, and you're more than a decoration on me, you question, make me think; you listen! The small dots are like leaves that drop, ripples that stop and dew drops that dry before noon."

"The small dots will grow on you, give them time. Patience, Pot."

"Patience? I see life in a whole new way now: sun rising on treetops, rooftops, next-door's swing set and slide, the up and down teeter-totter, around and around merry-go-round, clockwise this, counter-clock that."

"You see plenty already, good, but why not slow down a little?"

"Wait! By night there's even more: a cacophony of sound and an amalgam of life right at the edge of our ledge, beyond our sky, the verge of vast spaciousness seemingly ceasing to end. Darkness swallows darkness, forever, Indy."

"Wondrous, but spooky. The vast and the dark oughtn't make me sleepy, Pot, but they do."

"Don't be burdened, Indy; be enthralled."

"I'll try, just let me go back to sleep. To morning, Pot! Good luck with your dots."

"How can you sleep while dots punch and poke me? We all sleep on the same pot, and that's me!"

"I know how to quiet down, Pot, goodnight," and even deeper into Pot sinks Indy, flat with slumber. Inside Pot, the dots press and push. This time, Pot bends to their will, thinking shiatsu, and falls asleep, as the small blue dots eventually do, too.

Even in the still though, before morning's light, Pot startles awake. As the dots sleep, Pot watches them, their shine shows even in dark, their flat, round selves curled and clinging to Pot, artfully spaced but that Pot sees as sloppy. Pot wants dots with intent, no push or punch, pull or shove, dots that are just dots, not trouble makers and not needy. Pot wants excitement and adventure, while wondering where dots get their sense of play, from their indigo glaze? The potter? Or just being young dots? Who knows?

Outside, the song of a Golden-crown Sparrow prompts Pot to think about learning how to play with the dots inside, and tempers Pot's keen yen to get out. Pot thinks, "After Indy's awake, and I relax, I can learn how to play with at least a few of the dots," but the interrupting tap-tap-tap sound of a Red-breasted Sapsucker abruptly wakes Indy up.

"Good morning, Indy."

"It isn't morning. Outside I only see dark. Let me catch a few more winks. You're not headed for far-off adventure yet are you, Pot?"

"Not now, Indy," whose round indigo blue self sinks swiftly back to sleep, until the Morse-code chatter of a Ruby-crowned Kinglet morphs into song and awakens Indy anew, who asks what Pot's up to now. Indy listens to Pot's plan to relax and learn how to play with the small dots, even if only a few at a time, and gladdens so much as to set off at once to fetch some small dots.

Awaiting Indy's return, Pot remembers sounds of departing house visitors trailing their descent down the stairs to the sidewalk. Pot tunes in to words uttered by family near and far, by neighbors, writers and actors, scientists and engineers; words to move thought along to think and gather amid different thoughts, and Pot gladdens. Remembering their un-uttered wants and fears, Pot's feelings of gladness and sadness well up, taking feelings in the way clay takes in water. Pot retains others' uttered trials and travails, ecstasy and grief, and finds nourishment in them like plants with fertilizer, clay with lime, or soil with nitrogen. The longer Pot's heard words linger, and emotions turn air to cheesecloth filtering ups from downs, truth from exaggeration or lies, the more Pot can sense life, whether lived on two legs, a pair of crutches or a wheelchair, bearing beating hearts looking for love, looking at love, finding beauty and truth, and hope, or not, with Pot as witness and absorber.

"Pot, where are you? We're ready; did you go somewhere?"

"Indy, you have no idea. I'm feeling what it's like living here, visiting here, being a part of it, this house. Tell me about you, your life here."

"Pot, you have no idea. Living on our shelf shows me all about love and discord, near or far. Events here speak to me in volumes of food, candles and sconces, flowers and sideboards, paintings and wall pictures, and the long woven red tablecloth that tell about easy and hard, happy or not and, Pot, here are the best parts: dinners, parties, dancing, costumes, toasts and speeches, recitals and performances, people together on the landings, in the kitchen, and the rhythm and sound of music sparked by the drum. Once I hopped onto the drummers' busy fingertips to give a bit of a boost, but what's also good here is the comfort and gratitude in people's hearts and minds when mirth attends their sorrow."

"Wow, wherever you are, treasure finds you, Indy."

"I get about, don't I, Pot? Are you ready to play now? I have a few small dots waiting for you."

"To play in my mind, but nowhere else, not yet. May I have a rain check? I'm verklempt."

"Sure, Pot, but at least go and tell the two dots yourself who are waiting for you in the wings. Fair enough?"

"The wings, ah, like flying, of sorts."

"Yes, but one more thing, will you be going anywhere soon?"

"Of course I'm going somewhere, right here, with you, Indy."

"Well then, to the house, and you, Pot."

"And all of us in it!"

"Amen."

About the Contributors

Gigi Benson
Surviving the histrionics of an over-educated actress, Gigi's made a living onstage and off. Be it belting Shakespeare in the Pyrenees or marketing Manhattan bigwigs, this Wyoming weather girl from the Arizona desert was destined to meet the madcap maven Mae Meidav of Berkeley. Gigi's journey, road trip really, has taken its toll as any good adventure in life should. In fact, with Mae's insistence Gigi's been able to capitalize on Lady Bracknell's nightmare of *"a life full of incident."* Hauling a handbag worthy of Wilde's warped wanderings, she's taken the page to the stage, and sometimes back to the border, in her quest to leave things better than she found them, or at least liven them up. Truly blessed by her two sons, a million miracles and the bevy of bounty Brookside Writers has brought to her loosely liltyquake life, she looks forward to finding what others might see in her own jumbled journey. Each page turns in its own time — enjoy.

Dan Eeds is a retired accountant with the Association of Bay Area Governments, a novelist, and a world traveler. He has been a member of Mae Meidav's Brookside Writers Workshop since the mid-'90s. His novel *Columbus: Lost in Paradise* is a passion project. Dan recently completed Stanford Continuing Studies' two-year Novel Writing Program. His short story "Missadelphia 1961" was produced and performed as a one-act play for Notre Dame de Namur University Labor Day Festival (directed and co-produced by Brookside colleague Gigi Benson).

Michael C. Healy was an executive at the Bay Area Rapid Transit (BART) System heading up its Media and Public Affairs Department for 32 years. Not long out of college he was a contract writer for the old CBS radio drama, "Suspense," out of New York, and later managing editor of Marin Guide Publications, headquartered in Sausalito, California. Before joining BART he was at Paramount Studios in Los Angeles for a year, where he wrote a movie called "The Dirt Gang," which was released in 1971 worldwide by American International Pictures. Since retiring from BART he has written its history — *BART The Dramatic History of the Bay Area Rapid Transit System*, published in 2016 — and has written numerous feature stories for *Oakland* and *Alameda Magazines*. He's been a member of the Brookside Writers Workshop for almost 20 years. Mike makes his home in the Montclair District of Oakland with his wife Joan and dog Bella.

Brenda Kahn built a career in journalism and corporate communications while pursuing creative writing projects on the side, including a series of short one-act plays performed under the umbrella of the Brookside Writers Workshop. She has taught journalism/writing at City College of San Francisco and UC Berkeley's Goldman School of Public Policy, and her articles, op-eds and personal essays have appeared in the S.F. Chronicle, J. Weekly, Bay Woof and Bay Crossings, among other publications. Her brood of four children (including a set of identical twins) and family and workplace dynamics often provide material for her work. Brenda is on a never-ending quest to find and experience the world's best lap pool.

Edie Meidav is the author of the prose collection *Kingdom of the Young* (Sarabande), the novels *Crawl Space* (FSG) and *Lola, California* (FSG) among other work, including the recent lyric novel *Another Love Discourse (Terra Nova/MIT Press)*. Her work has been recognized by the Bard Fiction Prize and Kafka Prize, among other sites, and has received support from the Fulbright Program, the Howard Foundation, the Lannan Foundation and the Whiting Foundation. A senior editor at the journal *Conjunctions*, she is a professor in the MFA for Poets and Writers at the University of Massachusetts at Amherst.

Jeanne Perkins loves creating stories that are takeoffs on more justifiably famous works, such as her piece featuring a relative of Sherlock Holmes, taking the opportunity to take fresh looks at current events through the eyes of past authors. She also loves her Subaru, a character in her second story. But travel writing is her first love, hence the true story of a wildlife encounter. Her background as an earthquake hazard modeler and hazard mitigation planner drives her desire to write pieces that promote science. Jeanne has been a member of the Brookside Writers for over 20 years.

Mila Getmansky Sherman is professor of finance at the Isenberg School of Management, University of Massachusetts at Amherst. She is an expert on systemic risk, financial crises and financial institutions. She loves studying risk both in her professional and personal lives. She has published in academic and practitioner oriented publications. Mila is the newest member of the Brookside Writers.

Judith Silverstein was born in the early 1960s and never really figured out what to do after that. She has been a graduate student in Italian literature, an environmental policy researcher, and a laborer in the lower echelons of PR and journalism. Judith has been a member of the Brookside Writers Workshop since 2016, where she explores themes of failure and dysfunction, from awkward social moments to civilizational cataclysm. She survives in Berkeley, California.

Linda Walls loves her evenings with Brookside's weekly writing group: its space to think, riff and write, especially its opportunities to listen and learn, and reply and read her rapid writes aloud. When she can, Linda chooses transit over driving, and revels in singing (still) with the Anything Goes Chorus since '83. A retired secretary since Barack Obama was first inaugurated as the 44th president of the U.S., she is blessed with six siblings she would be the eldest of had her twin brother not beat her "out of the chute" three minutes before.

Made in the USA
Middletown, DE
09 January 2023

20926329R00151